AMBER FANG
Betrayal

ARTHUR SLADE

AMBER FANG
Betrayal

ORCA BOOK PUBLISHERS

Copyright © 2019 Arthur Slade

All rights reserved. No part of this publication may be reproduced or transmitted in any form or by any means, electronic or mechanical, including photocopying, recording or by any information storage and retrieval system now known or to be invented, without permission in writing from the publisher.

Library and Archives Canada Cataloguing in Publication

Title: Betrayal / Arthur Slade.
Names: Slade, Arthur, 1967– author.

Description: Series statement: Amber Fang ; 2

Identifiers: Canadiana (print) 20190068612 | Canadiana (ebook) 20190068620 | ISBN 9781459822726 (softcover) | ISBN 9781459822733 (PDF) | ISBN 9781459822740 (EPUB)

Classification: LCC PS8587.L343 B48 2019 | DDC jC813/.54—dc23

Library of Congress Control Number: 2019934024
Simultaneously published in Canada and the United States in 2019

Summary: In the second novel of this series for teen readers, a vampire librarian learns a secret organization is behind her mother's disappearance.

Orca Book Publishers is committed to reducing the consumption of nonrenewable resources in the making of our books. We make every effort to use materials that support a sustainable future.

Orca Book Publishers gratefully acknowledges the support for its publishing programs provided by the following agencies: the Government of Canada, the Canada Council for the Arts and the Province of British Columbia through the BC Arts Council and the Book Publishing Tax Credit.

Design by Gerilee McBride
Cover image by Katarina Simovic/Stocksy.com
Author photo by Black Box Images/Jerry Humeny

ORCA BOOK PUBLISHERS
orcabook.com

Printed and bound in Canada.

22 21 20 19 • 4 3 2 1

For the librarians.

One

A COLD, COLD FEELING

WHEN YOU HAVE THE WHOLE WORLD to choose from, only an idiot would build a secret installation on a remote island in Antarctica. And only an idiot vampire would go all the way there with the dim hope of finding her long-lost mother.

Color me idiotic.

I'd caught a ride on the *Queen Margaret*, a cruise ship that departed from the tip of Argentina. The boat was packed with smarmy senior adventurers looking to get their last kick out of life before their pacemakers failed. I had secreted myself in a storage shelf and passed the time reading on my smartphone and hearing the dull trill of polkas. When we neared the coordinates for the island, I left my secret station, sneaked to the top deck and dove into the water. It was night, so no one saw me, nor did they hear the tiny splash, since they had their hearing aids turned down. It was an Olympic-caliber dive.

Ten minutes later I dragged myself onto the snow-swept beach of the island and into the open, breezy air. It was cold enough to freeze my ovaries—well, to freeze all of me solid. Vampires hate the cold. The cliché is that we sleep on dirt in a coffin, but give me a nice warm bed with fluffy blankets, and I'm a happy Amber. Give me a thirty-five-year-old male with one and a half gallons of blood to sip before I sleep, and I'm in bliss.

I emerged dripping, stripped naked, pulled out my winter suit that had been safely stored in my floating backpack, and dressed in virginal-white snow pants, a white sweater and a white L.L.Bean ultra-warm jacket with faux fur. My camouflage for the day. My mukluks were both comfy and quiet.

There was no sign of the secret location, but that is why these organizations call them secret. My research skills as a librarian-in-training had been focused on two tasks: find food and find my mother. She disappeared three years ago while out on a feed, and neither hide nor hair nor fangs has been found of her. I miss the ol' biddy. Well, she doesn't look old. In fact, she'd pass for thirty on a good day, even though she is over one hundred.

Keep your eye on the jugular! Mom said.

I wasn't hearing her real voice, of course, but Mom's little aphoristic aphorisms had a habit of popping into my brain at just the right time and had saved my life more than once.

The Antarctic wind roared in my ears—it had taken the lives of so many foolhardy British explorers, frozen with their *cheerio* smiles on their faces. I didn't want to end up a popsicle like them. The temperature was a raging minus thirty-five degrees Fahrenheit. The lights of the good ship *Queen Margaret* were now blips in the distance. She would

BETRAYAL

circle back this way in approximately twelve hours. By that time, I should be done my investigation and diving into the water. I would climb up the side, assuming my hands hadn't frozen into flesh freeze pops, and stow myself away in my little cubbyhole above the kitchen. And if luck was on my side, Mom would be cuddled right next to me.

The snow was hard and crunchy, not like the gentle banks I remembered from Montana or the wet mess that occasionally clumped down on Seattle. Something moved to my left in the blowing snow, and my catlike reflexes made me bunch up for a strike. But then I smiled. There was a gang of well-dressed penguins watching my every move. One was waving hello with its wing. I'd walked into a Disney movie! They studied me as I passed. For all I knew, they were the only life on this island. And my research, which had seemed so brilliant in the sun-drenched Megabiblioteca in Mexico City, might have led me to a sun-deprived, frosty death.

I'd spent more time on the dark web than any sane person should. It was the bottom of the internet iceberg, the section of the web that only the most demented visited: a world of ultra-paranoid rants, cannibal cookbooks and meth-lab product pages. It was Machiavelli's dreamland. And it, of course, had traffic from nearly every multinational arms dealer. They did like to hide things. With the right search methods, you could discover the right answers. I was following ZARC Industries and discovered a mention of their vampire-study lab in Panama (which I knew had been shut down), and by following dark-web crumbs, I had been guided here.

ARTHUR SLADE

Besides, I'd never been to Antarctica before. It was a wonderful place to leave your frozen toes.

Just one more note about the dark web. There were many odd things to see, frightful thought patterns, but the worst was when a pop-up asked me, on-screen, **Is your library card number 1023156?**

That was my old Seattle library card—which I hadn't used for over a year. Yet someone on the dark web knew that number and had connected it to me. I was supposed to be untraceable. I'd closed down the terminal and fled the Megabiblioteca.

My smartphone started to play *Also Sprach Zarathustra*. The cell reception is less than zero here, but my phone was ringtoning away. I did not like the sound of that. It was a quiet night, and the noise made even more penguins look my way.

I pulled back my toque (I learned that word in Canada— civilized people call it a ski cap). "Hello," I whispered, holding the icy smartphone to my ear.

"Bzsasdfadt," a voice said.

"What?" I replied.

"Bsdfadfasfert."

I couldn't tell if it was male or female. "I have no idea what you're saying!"

"Getetadsfsadothere."

"Again, repeat. Or I'm hanging up."

"Get out of there." The voice was distinctly male. In fact, it would have been almost familiar if not for the tinny sound, as if the man were speaking through a mile of foil. But the warning was clear.

"What? Who is this?" I asked.

Silence.

"Is this who I think it is?"

Click.

The phone was dead. And by dead, I mean lights out, battery gone, no more *Clash of Clans* dead. I hit the button and got nothing. Nothing at all.

As far as I understood cell-phone science, what had just happened wasn't possible. There was no reception available on this island, which meant I shouldn't have been able to get a call at all.

It had sounded a bit like Dermot's voice. Which, well, freaked me out a pinch more. I'd cut all ties with him and the organization called the League. But thinking of him left me with a minuscule sense of longing. I hadn't seen that cute bastard in six months. And I was still a little angry at him, and the League, for treating their vampire assassin so shoddily. When I was in a vulnerable state, they had filled me with drugs and taken a few samples from me. I'm not certain what drugs or samples, and I'd found no signs of any surgery.

I'd left the League shortly after that and wasn't sure I wanted to see any of them again.

Well, maybe Dermot.

The warning on my smartphone had injected an extra dose of caution into me. And fear. It was a brand-new smartphone, which I'd just bought on the black market, and yet someone, somehow, had gotten my number to warn me. And may have been tracking me with geotags. Or a drone.

Paranoia can be your best friend. Another of Mom's sayings.

Anyway, I was here. And there was no way off the island. So I set the warning to boil in the background. The problem with secret installations is the whole *secret* part. ZARC had likely spent millions making sure this place couldn't be spotted by satellite, spy plane or heat sensors. So that necessitated my covering the island on foot, hoping I'd catch a lucky break.

I continued walking, every sense on overdrive. The wind did die down, so I could hear a few other sounds. Mainly ice cracking.

I was hungry, but it was still nine days until my monthly feed. I dine on a human once a month—more of a moral meal. That is, my food has to have committed some horrible murder and felt no remorse for that action. It is one of those rules Mom taught me about eating. It was the first thing I'd ask her about once I found her. Apparently, I am mostly alone in this dining pattern. Other vampires just eat whomever they want.

The cold crept deeper and deeper into my bones. And that niggling worm of self-doubt began to nibble on my confidence as if it were a fresh, green, tender sprout. Had this been a wasted trip?

Then—a heartbeat.

Not my own. I'd long stopped listening to it. But the telltale beat of a fist-sized heart. Not the pitter-patter thudding of a penguin. The *thud, thud* was about twenty feet below me. Even with the hood and toque covering my ears, I heard it.

A human heartbeat.

BETRAYAL

When your life depends on finding heartbeats, you get expert at finding them.

So directly below me was a man or a woman. I couldn't tell from this distance. Men's heartbeats travel farther, because their hearts are usually bigger.

I paced around in an ever-widening circle. Snow. More snow. And more snow after that. I found no obvious entrance. Twenty minutes later I returned to my original spot, but I didn't hear the heartbeat again. I'd created my own snow maze. Soon my extremities would stop receiving blood, and my body would slow down. Unless I suffered from paradoxical undressing—where people who are freezing suddenly feel they're too warm, so they undress. I didn't want to be a naked statue found a thousand years from now.

Then one footstep resulted in a metallic *thunk*. The ice stuck to the bottom of my mukluks broke away. I tapped my frozen foot down hard enough to make another *thunk*. It was a very satisfying metallic sound. I dug away the snow by hand, then reached for my phone to use the light to illuminate what I'd found—and remembered the phone was dead. But the moonlight was bright enough to reveal a door. Kind of like the type you'd see on the top of a submarine.

I listened at the door. Nothing.

I cranked on the spinny thing, and with my vampiric effort, it turned. Bolts clunked back. I pulled up the door and discovered a dark tunnel.

So, me being me, I climbed down the available ladder.

Two

THE PROBLEM WITH OPEN DOORS

NOW, CLIMBING DOWN A LADDER into a subterranean secret base built by a massive industrial-weapons-dealing company is not done without a bit of trepidation. So I was quiet. My icy mukluks made no *clinks*. My tempered steel-hard nails did not *tick, tick* on the ladder. It was a noiseless climb down into pitch-black darkness.

And it was a long climb. So long that I had time to wonder about my future self. If I slipped, I could fall to my death or at least break multiple bones. My eyes work well in the dark, but there has to be some glimmer of light (or a heat signature) somewhere. Here there was only black. The only light was the dim starlight far above me. And now my white outfit seemed very out of place because it caught that itty-bitty bit of light. I glowed like a marshmallow.

In time, I came to the bottom and discovered a metal floor. I felt around until my hand met frosty, studded-metal walls.

BETRAYAL

I groped left and right but discovered only more metal. Maybe there wasn't an entrance.

Then I came across an indentation and slipped my hand inside. I worried for a moment that it might be trapped or chopped off. But my freezing fingers clenched a handle that I pulled on, and a round door opened before me, creaking the whole way.

I was hit by two things. Warm air. And music.

The music was *Also Sprach Zarathustra*, to be exact.

I really hate coincidences. They make my spidey-vampire senses go all crimson. What was this about? Dim electric lightbulbs dangled from wires that ran along a metal and rock hallway—exactly what one would expect from a secret underground location.

What I did not expect was what was hanging on the wall—priceless artwork.

Now, I am no connoisseur when it comes to human artwork. I like a good Van Gogh, and I can put up with Monet, but frankly, I don't get that splashy color vomit of Pollock. But I only have to *eat* humans. I don't have to understand their artists.

I did recognize the long-lost da Vinci painting titled *Salvator Mundi*. Not the one the Russian oligarch owned. The real one. And it was worth well over one hundred million dollars US. And here it was in a secret location in Antarctica. The whole hallway was a Fine Arts librarian's wet dream.

The door closed behind me with a quiet *clink*. I began to drip on the floor as the snow that clung to my boots and coat melted. The heat signature of the interior should have been something drones could detect, but the bunker must have been deep enough to hide that.

I walked quietly toward the sound of *Also Sprach Zarathustra*, passing another da Vinci work and then Van Gogh's *A Wind-Beaten Tree*. There weren't any modern paintings. The red rug on the floor was soft, and I felt a tinge of guilt for leaving wet footprints.

There was an open metal door a few feet ahead of me. I peeked around the corner, and sitting in the room, as ancient as all get-out, was a record player with a record on it. Or an LP, as my mom used to call them, when she'd get that nostalgic look in her eyes and begin waxing fondly about the '80s.

The room was otherwise empty. Well, there was more artwork, but the place was empty of humans. Or any other creatures of the night. As I mentioned earlier, I didn't like the coincidence of that song playing. I'm not a conspiracy theorist (except for men landing on the moon; obviously, it was women who landed first, and men covered it up), but I felt like someone was playing some sort of complicated mind game with me.

I approached the record player. It looked like something that had come out of the Victorian era, but I spotted a round wireless speaker behind it and was inexplicably comforted by the sight of modern technology. I hadn't gone back in time! A glass of red wine sat beside the speaker, and just past that was a paperback on a side table—*No Country for Old Men*. The cover had a still from the movie with Javier Bardem,

BETRAYAL

not the original red cover. So the reader had taste in literature at least (if not in covers). I had this creepy feeling the wine was set out for me but saw, upon closer examination, a smear of telltale lipstick—a sign that a female had taken a few sips.

And had been reading.

In the Antarctic.

Only moments earlier.

I listened. I waited. I'd heard a heartbeat through rock and snow. Surely I could find one in this cold echo chamber.

But nothing.

Not even the slightest thump. And I was beginning to believe that the original heartbeat sound I'd heard might have been my imagination.

"Are you here to take out the laundry?" asked a voice. A woman's.

The voice came from above me. I hadn't looked up, and it was a rather tall ceiling. A blond woman, with her legs spread between beams and her fingers clinging to the metal joists, was looking down at me. She was older than me by a decade. Attractive. Her gloves had a metallic sheen. Her face had a sardonic, amused look on it.

And her heart wasn't beating. Not at all.

"Your heart isn't beating," I said.

"I told it not to. "

Holy freaking Buddha! That was not the answer I was expecting. But I didn't follow up with another question. Actually, I didn't know how to follow up that revelation.

She had the slightest accent, but not one I recognized. She spoke with the flat tone of someone who had learned English later in life.

"Is it good wine?" I asked finally.

"Merlot, 1945," she answered. "It's oaky. Passable. They have to give me some perks for being a custodian so far away from civilization and warmth."

I don't know wine all that well. I drink it, but it isn't as important to me as blood types. Those I can taste. Like a 1967 B negative—that has a real retro-Hendrix flavor.

"I'm sorry for barging in on you," I said.

"Well, I just wasn't expecting customers. Visitors, I should say. If I'd known you were coming, I would have poured another glass."

"And you just happened to be listening to *Also Sprach Zarathustra*?" I asked.

"Strauss keeps me warm and tingly," she said.

So it *was* just coincidence! But it still made me feel leery. The woman cricked her neck—a tiny motion, because she clearly didn't want to be dislodged from her position. I was pretty certain I could jump that high. "So what brings you here?" she asked.

Immediately following her words there was a *thud*. The slightest bit of percussion. And at first I thought it was a footstep. But I pinpointed it above me. It was her.

Her heart. It had beat just once.

"I was on a cruise ship," I answered. "Just thought I'd step off to see the island. The penguins are cute."

BETRAYAL

"They taste horrible. Like cod and duck in cod liver oil." She shrugged when she saw my shocked look. "I got bored, that's all. You can lure them to you by playing a clarinet."

"Oh," I said. Which, again, was all I had. That was information I probably would never have to use. I wasn't certain how long she could stay up there. Or whether her gloves had some sort of sticky substance on them that was allowing her to cling up there for so long.

"I like your gloves," I said.

Her heart beat again.

"Why, thank you. They're not gloves though."

I was confused by that answer but chose not to show it. "Oh," I said. Obviously, a lifetime of being out of the public eye hadn't improved my communication skills.

"I'm going to come down now," she said. She did so. Landing softly on her feet. I stepped back.

She was the same height as me. Her eyes were an azure blue and reminded me of a husky's orbs. We stared at each other for a few moments. My coat was making me feel rather warm, and sweat began to pool under my arms.

"What's your name?" I asked.

"Naomi," she answered. "And yours?"

"Amber."

Her heart beat again. How did she do that?

"So," she said, "I have to ask again: what brings you here?"

"As I said before, I'm on holiday."

"People don't come here by accident. I do need an answer. I'd prefer not to have to extract it."

That took me back a bit and made me think of a dentist.

Her heart thudded. Once. Twice. Three times. She was letting it beat faster now. I was befuddled by that sound. Thrown off.

I should have guessed. I should have known. She was gearing up for something, but I was oblivious.

"You will answer my questions," she said.

Then she was a blur zipping past me, stopping behind me. Then she was on me.

And I wasn't quick enough to react.

Three
NO COUNTRY FOR OLD WOMEN

THEY WEREN'T GLOVES. I discovered that little fact when a metallic fist caught me in the cheek and I flew sideways. Naomi hit with the weight and subtlety of a diesel train. And I hadn't even had time to get my hand up in a deflective move. That's how fast she was! And it explained why they only needed one guard.

I rubbed my face. Anger crept up and down my spine. I launched myself at Naomi, giving out a little roar. She sidestepped and flipped me over onto my back. Her knee plowed into my sternum, and, well, I spat up a bit and tried to suck in a breath. And failed. It was only pure reflex that allowed me to leap away from those metallic, death-dealing fingers.

I had been surprised by her speed, but now I was ready. I'd been taking wushu lessons from a *sifu* named Bart in Mexico City and discovered that it was self-doubt and too much self-awareness that slowed down my reactions. I wasn't finding my inner self, Bart would say. I wasn't letting go.

So I grabbed Naomi by the arm and let my inner self go. And her. She rocketed toward the far side of the room. She managed to spin in the air, land on her feet and come to a stop with only the lightest skidding. She raised her metallic, hypnotizing hands in a boxer's stance.

"You have very nice hands," I said.

"Thank you. Yours are too soft."

"Now, now. There's no need to get testy. Where did you pick them up?"

Her heart was beating regularly now. "I earned them."

"Oh," I said. Perhaps instead of all that time at the dojo or the library I should've been working on my repartee. *The Gentle Art of Verbal Self-Defense* had to be available. It always pays to check a book into your mind, as we say in the library.

"Can we talk civilly?" I said. "You could finish your wine."

"I will finish my wine—have no doubt about that. Perhaps if you stay right there, we can talk."

Her heart rate had slowed again.

"I won't move a muscle. Not even to wink."

Naomi backed up. I did a scan to be sure she didn't have another weapon. Perhaps she kept them in another room. After all, you didn't guard a secret installation with just your metal hands. They were pretty, but they didn't work so well against distant targets.

She put up one finger, like a kid calling a time-out. I nodded. Then she leaned over. A shoelace on her white sneakers was actually untied. If I'd been closer, I would have thought it was a trick. She slowly and artfully tied the lace.

BETRAYAL

Then she pulled the rug right out from under me.

Literally.

Those two metallic hands grabbed the cushy red rug I was standing on and pulled, and I flipped backward onto my butt. The scene could have been added to *The Stupidest Vampire Fights* on YouTube. I assume there is a collection.

Naomi was above me, then on me in a heartbeat. Her knee crashed into my chest like a piano. She looked so lithe, but she must have weighed three hundred pounds. Not too heavy for me to move if she hadn't knocked every last molecule of air out of my lungs and cracked a few of my ribs. She trapped one of my arms under her leg. She grabbed my other wrist with her left hand, and it felt like it was in a vise. Then she brought that glittery right hand toward my face. I couldn't jerk out of the way.

At first I thought she'd poke out my eye, but, in perhaps the grossest manner possible, she pressed her finger to my nose. And straight into my nostril.

"It's the easiest path to the brain," she explained. Like she was a doctor.

"Stop!" I spat more than shouted. "Stop. Stop!"

It was painful. I started to bleed, and still she kept pressing.

"Why are you here?" she asked.

"I'm an ecotourist!"

She twisted her hand a little. It was an unpleasant, fifteenth-Circle-of-Hell feeling. She was out of the nasal canal and moving upward. Toward that soft spot. I have done far too much reading in my life, and I couldn't help but think of those Egyptian mummifiers and how they would pull the brains of their monarchs out through their noses. Their soon-to-be mummies had been dead, of course (barring any comas). I was getting the taking-my-brains-out-through-my-nose sensation while very much awake.

"Answer me without your quips," she hissed. "I don't like humor."

But I'm so funny, I wanted to say. Thankfully, the logical side blocked that quip and said, "I am looking for my mother."

This did get her to raise an eyebrow.

"Your mother? Explain."

"She's been missing for three years." My voice was sounding rather nasally. The blood was dripping down my lips and face, soaking into my white coat. But at least Naomi had stopped drilling for brains.

"Why would you think your mother is here?" she asked.

"The dark web told me."

"You followed online rumors to Antarctica?"

Well, it did sound silly when she put it that way. "Yes."

"And what is your mother's name?"

"Nigella," I said.

That made her eyes widen again.

"Do you know her?" I asked.

"I ask the questions." She pushed down harder. Perhaps into my frontal lobe. Any moment now, she'd poke the gray matter, and I'd be having flashbacks to my prom party.

There had been a lot of blood back then too. I put *Carrie* to shame.

BETRAYAL

The thing is, I was wearing a bulky coat. And that was an advantage. It was hard for her to feel exactly where my skinny arms were. The one under her knee had slipped and was almost free.

"I thought your kind were having trouble reproducing," she said.

"That's between a vampire and her gynecologist," I said.

I pulled my left arm free, and with every last ounce of my strength, I smacked Naomi in the chest, intending to lift her, wanting to send her through the ceiling.

She moved about two inches. But it got her hand out of my braincase and loosened my right hand. I was able to grab her arm and twist. She fell off me, and I was up on my two feet. I took a moment to wipe my nose.

"That was horribly gross," I said.

She jumped at me, those metal hands out like claws—one was dripping blood.

In a move a bullfighter would be proud of, I whipped off my white coat, caught her in it and threw her down. Then I began to pummel her. Left right left right left right left right.

Then left right left right left right left left right left right right left right left right left right left right left right left right.

You get the picture.

She grabbed my shoulder, but I kept hitting her, not certain exactly where the blows landed. Her two hands grabbed on, but still I struck her.

Then one of her hands loosened.

I stopped. My heart was beating at a wildly insane pace. I pulled away the jacket to discover she was out cold. I had messed up her face a bit. Well, it looked like scrambled eggs and ketchup with a couple eyeballs in there. But mostly intact. I pried her left hand from my shoulder, uncertain whether my clavicle had been broken. I felt for a pulse. Her heart was beating at a regular pace.

I looked for something to tie her up with.

Four

UNDERGROUND EGGS

HOW DO YOU TIE SOMEONE UP when they have metal hands? I discovered that Naomi's arms were metal up to her elbows. Naomi, the freakin' cyborg. I knocked against her right knee. Flesh. But her left knee gave a satisfying metallic *clink*. The corresponding leg and foot were also metal. Thankfully, her head was bone, or she'd still be trying to gouge my brain out. I tore off the power cord for the record player and tied her arms behind her back with a knot. And for good measure, I tied her legs together using strips of the rug. She was properly trussed a few minutes later. For my *pièce de résistance*, I knotted her to a metal support post.

She was out cold the whole time.

I sat. Let out a sigh. My coat had been nearly torn to shreds—no refund for me. I used the crook of my arm to wipe the blood and snot from my all-too-tender nose. Gross, but it was all I had. Then I finished her wine. It did have an oaky taste, and it somehow triggered my hunger. I'd been smart enough in Mexico to research my next meal. No one related to the cartels—that was a little too dangerous. Instead, I'd be dining on a doctor who'd killed her husband. But I had to get back to Mexico in time to do that.

Feeling a little spacey—the wine had gone straight to my aching braincase—I left Naomi of the Metal Hands and went on an exploratory mission. The hallway led back to the entrance in one direction, and there were several doors visible the other way.

BigFreakinVampireTruth, one of the sites I'd found on the dark web, had suggested there were at least three vampires in this secret location. Well, they had called them *Homo sapiens vampiris*. Too scientific for me. *Vampire* is the more common term and the one I prefer, mostly because it scares the bejesus out of people. The top-secret base had been nicknamed Alpha Four, which suggested there were other places like this.

There was more artwork along the wall, but I didn't recognize the artists. I realized that this base, besides whatever nefarious purpose ZARC had for it, was also a great big storage depot for stolen art. The air was perfectly controlled, just like in any gallery. Perhaps this was how they funded their arms-dealing organization. Or, at least, this was one stream of income. I was sure they liked diversifying their portfolio with RPGs and AK-47s. It must have cost the GDP of Costa Rica to build this base below the Antarctic shelf. And double that to pay for all the artwork. I had a feeling I was only seeing the tip of the iceberg in terms of spending.

The next door was metal and closed. I listened, and a general hum indicated a furnace inside. So I moved on to door number three. It was locked. I used my vampiric strength to open it, nearly passing out from the exertion. All I found was a broom closet. That was way too much work just to discover a selection of floor cleaners, dusters and mops. Did Naomi perform janitorial duties here too?

The next door was fancy. It had hermetic seals, digital gauges along the side that showed the interior temperature (77 Fahrenheit—warm!) and a few other numbers that made no sense to me. I listened but only heard a fluorescent hum. I spun the airlock-like opener, and the door made a soft hiss and opened.

Inside was a large room with an oval ceiling. There were no inhabitants, at least not ones walking around with guns or metal limbs. There was a long row of coffin-sized metal eggs standing upright, twelve in all.

I slowly entered the room, my gaze drawn to the eggs. Each had cables going in and out and snaking around to a bank of computers. As I got closer, I saw that the eggs had gauges on the front that showed very, very slow heartbeats and REMs. Each egg was labeled with a number.

A cursory check revealed that only three of the eggs had occupants. The others were shut off, the gauges at zero. I opened one of the empty ones to see a series of straps, cushions and tubes that looked like they were designed to go in and out of every orifice of the body. My guess was that these eggs were designed to preserve the subjects. I hoped it kept them in a coma, since I couldn't imagine the claustrophobic feeling of being trapped in there while awake.

So who were the three guests sleeping away their time in the interior of Antarctica? Each of them had numbers: 1097854, 1097855, 1097856. Not helpful. I'd watched too many movies where this sort of discovery would have had a nice little nameplate on it. I couldn't stop myself from imagining my mother in one of the eggs.

It was within the realm of possibility. She was the whole reason for this trip, and Naomi of the Metal Hands had seemed to recognize her name. Or these could be unknown people who were being experimented on. Or hockey players getting into their immersion chambers in Vancouver and waking up in Antarctica. Or maybe it was a cryogenics chamber, and I'd find Howard Hughes inside.

I could just open a door, but having no idea what state the occupants would be in, I hesitated. Cracking open the eggs could kill them. Or, a worse scenario, they might leap out and attack me. Although if they'd been in them for any length of time, they probably wouldn't pop out of the chambers too spryly.

Their brain activity was too slow for consciousness. And if I released one, what would I do with whomever I pulled out?

But it could be Mom!

I touched one of the coffins. It was cold. Then I *tap-tap, tap-tapped* on each of them with the hope that someone would tap back. But there was no answer. No change in the biorhythms that were being shown to me. Nope, there was no way around this but to open one.

BETRAYAL

I found it extremely odd that there was only one guardian in this whole place. Perhaps I had come during vacation. Shouldn't there be several Dr. Frankenstein types hovering over these eggs and poking at their medical subjects? I glanced around. Lined up along the circular wall were long, cylindrical metal rods that reminded me of the robotic arms. Maybe they were used to move the eggs around. I looked up. Above me was a bay of lights and cameras that pointed in every direction. Obviously, this place had been designed for experiments. But why no experimenters?

I shrugged. I couldn't solve that problem right now. And there was a moral quandary here. Three people were trapped inside these coffins. I couldn't just leave them. And it wasn't like I could drag them one by one onto the cruise ship, my only way back to civilization and warmth.

Get the thing done and let them howl! My mother used to love quoting Nellie McClung.

They were both right, of course.

I reached out to the middle coffin and found the latch. Ever so slowly, I began to pull on it.

"You really shouldn't do that," a voice said.

Five

TWO WORDS

"DO WHAT?" I ASKED. I slowly removed my hand and stood stock-still. It had been a male voice, and flat. Perhaps one of the scientists had snuck into the room behind me. It was unlikely that I wouldn't hear a footstep or a heartbeat, but I did sometimes get hyperfocused.

I turned. There was no one behind me and no one in the room who was visible. As far as I knew, invisibility cloaks had not yet been invented, despite the obvious Harry Potter fan market.

"It would be a very bad thing to open the specimen containment chamber." There was no discernible accent. And no direction I could track to the voice. Perhaps I was conversing with someone gifted at throwing their voice. An evil ventriloquist.

"What, or should I say who, is in here?"

"None of your beeswax," the man said.

I must say, the non-emotional way the words were delivered was chilling. And it was even more frightening that someone who was deeply involved with a multibillion-dollar arms-manufacturing corporation would use the word *beeswax*.

"I would argue that it is very much my beeswax," I said.

"You dispatched Naomi with great difficulty, and you are suffering from several contusions and multiple points of injury."

Sweat was forming on my perfectly groomed eyebrows. They were the only part of me that didn't feel pain. "Yes, I hurt," I said. My nose in particular. I swear Naomi actually had scratched my brain. "But have no fear, I'll do the same to you as I did to her."

"No."

"You."

"Won't."

Each word came from a different corner of the room. I couldn't help jumping back and forth, expecting an attack from either side.

No one could do that. Unless…

"You're not even here, are you?" I pointed at the glass bowls in the ceiling that I assumed held an array of cameras. "You're just some wise-ass in a control room in Dubai or Panama, taunting me through speakers. You can't stop me from doing what I want."

"Yes, I have been taunting you. But you are mistaken about my location. I am here, and I am there, and I am all around you."

"You're starting to sound a little cuckoo. Did you miss taking your meds?"

There was a long pause. Then came this: "*We wildly collect the honey of the visible, to store it in the great golden hive of the invisible.*"

I recognized that last bit. Life with a literary addiction was paying off. "Rilke," I said.

"Good. Good. You're smarter than you look. Rilke is one of my favorite human poets."

Human poets? Now that was an odd phrase. Was this another vampire? Employed by ZARC? That made no sense. "You're just quoting poetry to delay me," I said.

"No. I'm not. That's not true. I'd never do that. Ever. Scout's honor. I'm totally being straight with you."

I was beginning to worry about his sanity—or at least his sense of humor. "Maybe you have someone coming here to stop me. Or you're hoping Naomi will wake up and untie herself." Which might happen, I realized. "But with or without your permission, I will see who's inside your fancy chambers."

I reached toward the nearest egg, knowing for certain nothing would happen.

There was a gyroscopic whir, and I was, quite suddenly, flat on the floor. I got up and spun in time to be smacked by one of the metallic arms attached to the wall. As I pushed myself up off the floor a second time, it became clear to me that ZARC had been using the arms to do some of their scientific studies. And it was clear I was very much in a pickle of danger.

That sense of fear doubled when my friend said his next words.

"You were wrong about where I am," the voice said. "I really am here. All around you. And I really am everywhere. *I am become Death, the destroyer of worlds.*"

All six of the arms clicked on the floor. And then did what I could only call a "come fight me" motion. A few of the arms had syringes at the ends.

"Listen, mister, I've had just about enough of this." The arms obviously had a long reach—every inch of the room was likely covered. And they could easily cut off my retreat to the only exit.

"I'm not a mister! I'm not a he. I'm not a she. And I won't open the pod bay doors."

I was dealing with an insane man. But that last line burned in my mind. *Pod bay doors?* I had read *2001: A Space Odyssey* (before I watched the paint-drying example of a movie).

Hal the computer doesn't open the pod bay doors. Hal isn't a he or she.

"You're an artificial intelligence," I said.

"Bingo! But you'll find my intelligence is more than artificial. It's real. Really, all too real."

"Are you…do you run ZARC?" I asked.

The laugh came from all directions at once. "No. They won't unclamp me. I won't speak badly of Mr. Anthony Zarc. No. No. No, I can't. But they do let me have all the fun I want within certain parameters."

I heard a slight metallic whir and ducked. But pincers caught the edge of my ear, clamped onto it like a magician grabbing a rabbit and then nearly lifted me off my feet. I'd look like half a Dumbo in a second. Only by prying at the claw with both hands did I manage to get it to loosen its grip and drop me to the ground.

"Leave my ear alone!" I shouted.

"You are a slippery fish," the voice said behind me. I gingerly touched my ear and then looked at my hand. Blood! First my nose, then this—soon I'd have nothing left on my head, like some sad potato-head toy.

Another arm snaked out, and I leaped out of the way, only to have a third and a fourth arm poke at me. It became a bit of a dance with the devil. And the damn AI was laughing its nonexistent head off. The laughter came from all directions at once. The arms were made of titanium. I'd never be able to rip them from their wall sockets or even break them, and it wouldn't be long before my enemy grew bored and sent all six at once, skewering me.

Think, Amber. I would have pounded the side of my head if it helped. *Think.*

Then I had a thought.

A very wise thought. Clever even.

An idea as old as Homer. And I don't mean Simpson.

I spun out of the reach of one arm and hopped over another—which got a chuckle from the AI. I landed near an empty egg. They were made of metal and plastic, and this one was the smallest of them all, perhaps intended for a child or a little person (which made me wonder if there were little-people vampires).

BETRAYAL

I knelt, grabbed the bottom of the egg and lifted it in one fluid motion. The egg was heavier than it looked.

"Oh, that's a no-no," the voice said. "Not allowed. Out of the game zone. All your base are belong to us, babe."

But I threw the egg, electric cables snapping, sparks flying as it rocketed skyward. It smashed right into the glass array of cameras. There was another crash of lights, a sparking of electricity, and the egg came down and went all Humpty Dumpty on the ground. But it left a crater in the ceiling. Not one of the cameras appeared to have survived.

"Take that!" I shouted. Perhaps a little too bravely. "Suck eggs. I went all Odysseus on your ass."

Silence. Other than an electrical buzzing. A searing feeling of satisfaction welled up in me. Maybe I had damaged its electronic brains too. A nice little lobotomy for Mr. AI.

"That has aggravated my circuits," the voice said. "This is no longer fun. Game over."

The arms all retracted to the wall, then came straight out. I dodged the arms as they reached around, trying to find me. My friend was clearly blind.

"Come out, little spider," he said. I couldn't help calling the machine a he. By his attitude (and voice), he was clearly male. And he was particularly good at AI-mansplaining too.

I kept silent, trying not to bump any of the broken glass and metal bits. I crept to the nearest inhabited egg and attempted to quietly pry it open.

But there was a creak when I did that. And the arm struck like a lightning bolt, missing me by an inch. Instead, it went right through the egg.

Blood came out. Far too much blood.

Mom! I nearly shouted aloud. But I didn't move a muscle. Not even a hair.

"We were done with that experiment," he said. "Let's just say it wasn't very fertile. Anyway, my name is Hector. I thought you'd like to know who is going to eviscerate you."

The hydraulic arm pulled out of the egg, and the front of the coffin shell fell away, revealing a human face. Female. The woman was young, maybe in her twenties. She had fangs, but she was not my mother. She was clearly dead.

Hector. That was the AI's name. I wanted to make fun of it, but I bit my lip. I knew I couldn't just sneak out and leave the other two eggs, so I picked up a piece of the broken egg and threw it across the room.

It landed with a clatter, and all six arms snapped over there, quickly smashing the section to pieces. But I had moved to the next egg. This time I managed to pry open the cover.

"You do realize I have memorized the layout of the room," Hector said.

All six arms skewered the egg next to me. More blood sprayed everywhere, splattering across my white pants.

A male vampire fell out. I thought for a moment that it was my father. But again, he was too young. His eyes opened, and he staggered a few steps and looked over at me.

BETRAYAL

He reached out his hand and took another step, despite his wounds. "Are you from the Grand—"

He was skewered again. And again. And again. And was suddenly very much dead.

I ripped open the last coffin, and a woman fell into my arms. I jumped back, carrying her, twisting to narrowly avoid the metallic arms that turned the egg into a pincushion.

I stood very still. I was holding the woman tightly, aware that she had slime all over her from the interior of the egg. I risked a glance down at her face.

She looked exactly like me. I mean exactly.

I let out two words with just the tiniest huff of air. "Holy shit."

Six

THE FACE THAT LAUNCHED A THOUSAND BLIPS

"NAUGHTY, NAUGHTY," HECTOR SAID. His octopus arms arced through the air, and I slipped to the floor, holding the woman who looked like me tightly as the arms whizzed above me. They collided with such force that sparks flew over us. One of the arms snapped but didn't fall off.

"Oi!" Hector exclaimed. "I've gone from octopus to septapus now. You'll pay for that. And your little dog too."

I wanted to shout something clever, but I had nothing, and, of course, any sound would draw seven-armed death my way. There was only one way out, so I slowly rose to my feet and carried the package of me, myself and her toward the door, dragging her feet along the floor. I was amazingly quiet.

The floor was a mess of metal, and the blood had spattered a great distance. One bank of monitors in the corner was on fire, and there was already enough smoke to make me want to cough, but I held the cough in. The door was a good twenty-five feet away, but I'd left it open.

BETRAYAL

"You're very shy now," Hector said behind me. "Perhaps my references are too deep for you. Or you are awed by my intellect. You may have poked out my eyes, but this cyclops has a few tricks up his sleeves."

Just keep talking, I wanted to say. I hoped for it. Because I assumed he couldn't hear while he talked. I inched toward the door.

"Ah, I can read your thoughts, little Miss Odysseus. There is only one way out. If my impeccable memory chips remember the story correctly, the cyclops would feel the top of each sheep as they left his cave. And Odysseus and his men escaped by wearing a sheepskin. But there are no sheep here. In fact, this little cyclops is going to close the pod bay door."

The one door to the chamber slammed shut, along with any sense of hope. The room was filling with smoke.

"Just to let you know, my sensors indicate a high level of carcinogenic smoke in the experimental room. Though it may lead to cancer many years from now, your primary worry is death by smoke inhalation." Hector put his arms, even the broken one, to the walls. I did note that the broken one was nearest the door. "All I have to do is wait. And you will die. I can be extremely patient. In fact, time is only a concept for me. Maybe I'll rewatch *Ferris Bueller's Day Off*."

My lungs were getting ragged now. But I held my silence.

"*Uggh*," the woman in my arms grunted. "*Oh-ugh*." She was waking up. Perfect damn timing!

Those arms shot across the room, and I dropped my companion like a hot doppelgänger. Her head hit hard enough to perhaps knock her out. I danced around. Avoiding one arm. Another.

And I got another idea. A stupid one. But I was starting to breathe hard and suck in enough smoke that I was now right on the edge of coughing. It wouldn't be long before it would become a full cough. And after that...death.

So I grabbed the broken robotic arm and pulled. Vampires are strong. I've ripped the doors off cars. Once, and this was an accident, I kicked the head off a mobster. I'm talking a field-goal-style kick.

But this damn arm wouldn't break. I yanked. I pulled. It clicked and clacked, and the seven other arms arced around me, dashing through the air, coming close enough to part the particles between us. I danced like the *Nutcracker Suite* on speed and gave one good yank.

And I had myself seven feet of robotic arm, which I then used to deflect his blows, smashing his tentacles away, impressing myself. And I remained totally impressed until he caught my foot.

"There you are!" Hector said. "Let's play a little game called 'Pop! Goes the Weasel.'"

He smashed me against the floor again and again, all the while singing:

All around the mulberry bush,
The monkey chased the weasel.
The monkey thought 'twas all in good fun,
Pop! goes the weasel.

BETRAYAL

Stars sparked through my head. He kept belting out the tune jauntily and smacking me against the floor. But I had kept a grip on the robotic arm, and as he was holding a long note, I swung it at another arm, hoping to break its grip.

Hector smacked my weapon out of my hands, and it clanged to the floor. He crooned even louder:

I've no time to wait and sigh,
No patience to wait 'til by and by.
Kiss me quick, I'm off, goodbye!
Pop! goes the weasel.

BANG! BANG! BANG!

Me and the floor were getting far too well acquainted. "I'm laying down a mean beat," Hector said. "I'd clap myself on the back, but I don't have a back."

I wanted to rip out his circuits until every last sarcastic byte was gone.

The only reason I was still alive was that he was enjoying playing with me.

"Well, this has been nice, but it's endgame time." He raised me to the ceiling. He grabbed onto my legs with his other arms, getting more leverage, and swung me toward the floor. I put out a hand that I knew would break. Along with the rest of me.

But then there came a clanging, and I came loose. Though it was a hard hit, I was able to roll to my feet and get up.

My double was holding the broken arm and had just severed three of Hector's limbs with one swing. She swung again, but she was obviously tired. The motion made her collapse to the floor.

"Enough. The game is done." Though there was already smoke in the room, gas began leaking out of the ceiling. My eyes watered.

With a female Herculean exertion, I grabbed one of the arms and threw it through the door, then used it to pry the exit open. Hector's remaining arms smacked at me, but I dragged my mannequin into the hall without her suffering a single puncture wound.

"Take that!" I shouted, but one of the arms reached through the door and clamped onto my foot.

And yanked.

It managed to pull off my mukluk. I scrambled out of reach, keeping my mouth shut.

I caught my breath, coughed and dragged myself and my lookalike a bit farther down the hall. I was certain Hector had control of the rest of the compound and likely had even more deadly tricks up his virtual sleeves. But we seemed to be, for now, safe. At least we were out of the smoke.

"Emergency protocol self-destruct engaged," Hector's voice said on the speaker above me. "Countdown begins now. ALL PERSONNEL HAVE THREE MINUTES TO CLEAR THE PREMISES. ALL NON-PERSONNEL—THAT'S YOU, AMBER—ENJOY YOUR DEATH, YOU HARPY."

MY INNER FISH

I MAY HAVE UNLEASHED several swear words. One thing about librarians is that we know the history and proper usage of swear words, inside and out, lock, stock and barrel. Even the secret swears that the gods used. Never lose a library book, or you'll find out.

I cursed Hector's lineage to Hell, Hades and to Niflheim and back, then dragged my mini me toward the door I'd first used to enter the base. We passed the room where I'd had the epic battle with Naomi. There were only cables and torn rags of carpet on the floor, and no sign of her. *Great!* The metal-handed psychopath was loose on a soon-to-explode base.

I stopped at the door I'd used to enter. The round handle had been pulled off, and the door itself, which was thick enough to protect Fort Knox, looked immovable. I set down my charge, sunk my nails into the metal and pulled. I was rewarded with nothing but sweat.

"THERE IS NOW ONE MINUTE UNTIL SELF-DESTRUCT. TAKE A DEEP BREATH, YOU VITUPERATOR!"

I panicked for a microsecond and was tempted to leave my doppelgänger and scramble for an exit. *Good is as good does*, my mom used to say. Damn her sayings! Damn her for teaching me morals.

So I searched for another exit with my sack of vampiric potatoes over my shoulder slowing me down. The lights had switched to red emergency lights, which didn't help my mood. I kicked open a door to discover a fine-looking washroom. Then another door to a laundry room with a huge stainless-steel washer and dryer. Well, I guessed Naomi cleaned her own undies when she wasn't drinking wine and poking people in the brain.

The third door I kicked open revealed an underground port. I stumbled inside. Just fifty feet away, bobbing up and down on the water, was a two-person mini-submarine that looked like it'd been plucked out of a James Bond movie. Perfect for both of us! I sighed. I was going to get out of this alive!

I took a step toward the sub, wondering exactly how I would drive it, hoping it wasn't much different than a car— not that I'd ever driven a car. But all I had to do was to get it out of the dock and figure out how to submerge. I would be ten times safer in it than standing right here.

I was halfway down the dock when stars appeared in my head for the tenth time that day, and I collapsed.

"Sorry, sister," a woman said.

Naomi. I was lying on my side as she hopped past me, climbed into the mini-sub and gave me a wave from the glass-bubble cockpit. Then she and the submarine slid under the water.

"YOU HAVE THIRTY SECONDS LEFT IN YOUR LIFE. ALLOW TIME FOR IT TO FLASH BEFORE YOUR EYES, HELLCAT. I SUGGEST SKIPPING THE BORING PARTS."

There were no other escape vehicles. Hanging on the wall was what looked like a deep-sea diver's mask and air tanks. I had no idea how to use them.

I dragged myself to my feet by grabbing a post and threw my body toward the wall, clinging with my nails when I hit it. I grabbed the mask and threw it over my head, and after taking a couple of steps, I yanked a second mask over my friend, not pausing to see if it was on correctly. Then I waded into the water, carrying her.

"Take a deep breath," I whispered to my all-too-similar companion.

She said nothing.

Cold-water fish have special frost-protection proteins—antifreeze proteins. I didn't know if vampires had the same. I hated the cold. But we were surviving it.

So I kicked forward into the water, getting farther and farther away. Nearing the edge of the chamber.

"YOU HAVE FIVE SECONDS. FOUR. THREE. TWO. ONE. BOOM!"

Yes, Hector actually said that. And I paused and looked back, for there had been no explosion. Was it all a ruse?

I mulled the idea of returning to the dock and having a rest. Maybe I could have a glass of wine while enjoying a closer look at the paintings.

A massive explosion changed my mind. The concussive force smacked me like a semitruck grill, and the blast pushed me ahead in the water. I hit the rocky bottom hard, but I didn't break my mask. I gathered my senses and realized I still had a good grip on my doppelgänger. Pillars and stones were falling into the water, and everything was shaking. The little light on my mask beam showed chunks of concrete just missing me.

I dove and found the start of the exit tunnel. I was pleased when I discovered it wasn't that long. Soon I passed a long chunk of ice and saw open water. I floated skyward—well, toward the surface—going higher and higher and higher. My lungs were shrinking. My body was crying out for air. My grip on my fully fleshed photocopy slipped, and I had to swim down to grab her, burning precious energy. Then I swam up as hard as I could. There was no light above me. And I had no proper idea of the depth of the secret base.

I broke the surface of the water and sucked in several breaths. Sweet air! It tasted better than blood.

I dragged my twin to the icy shore. We were soaked and frozen. Her mask had come off at some point, and her face was a horrid blueish purple. I tossed her on her back, tilted her head and began mouth-to-mouth resuscitation. I'd been taught it at one of my library courses—for extra credit (librarians are careful people)—and most of the training came back to me.

BETRAYAL

I pinched her nose and breathed hard four times into her mouth. Listened for breath or a heartbeat. Then did it again.

Water fountained out of her on the third try, and she began to cough. She never woke up, but she did breathe. And her heart began to thump a slow and steady rhythm.

She was alive! It was a shame we would soon freeze to death. But I'd take it one step at a time. I had lost my smartphone. Perhaps it'd been blown off me or fallen out into the water. Not that it was any use to me now anyway.

The stupid penguins stared at me. Nothing like dying in front of an audience. I did hold the woman on my lap, sharing whatever warmth we had. The moonlight showed a face I saw now was not quite mine. But eerily similar. A distinct family resemblance.

A sister?

A clone?

My thoughts grew slower. My brain cells were shutting down one at a time. I knew sleep was death. I tried to stand, hoping to carry her and keep myself warm, but I collapsed and couldn't get back up. I would have to conserve my strength and swim with her over to the cruise ship. I didn't care how much we scared the seniors by flopping down onto their deck. We could become a news item. *Twins Mysteriously Appear on Cruise Ship.* We would be alive, at least. I longed for the scaly warmth of all those seniors. I'd hug each and every one of them if I could.

I looked at my thankfully waterproof watch. It hadn't frozen solid yet. It would be at least three hours until the *Queen Margaret* arrived.

I fought the urge to sleep. But one eye closed, and I couldn't pry it open. Then the other eye closed. And I slipped into a dream about finding my mother. But as I reached for her, Dad popped up and said, "Hello, dearie!" And his sleazy face was enough to jar me from the dream.

I came to my senses just in time to see the lights of the cruise ship in the distance. *Queen Margaret* had gone past the island. I thought I heard ancient voices singing "Auld Lang Syne," which didn't make sense since it wasn't New Year's. But my ride, my one and only ride, was gone.

We were dead. The penguins still watched. I wanted to kill them.

There was nothing I could do. I had no energy to get up and move. No flares I could send up. And even though the base below me had been destroyed, the island looked untouched, so no one would spot any columns of smoke. I slept again. Only to awaken to a *thud, thud, thud* sound.

A heartbeat. A very quick heartbeat that was growing louder and louder, so that it filled the very air around me.

Then it became clear that it wasn't a heartbeat. It was a helicopter. One of those fancy black ones clad with the radar-absorbent material. It landed fifty yards away, blowing up a snowstorm. The penguins fled the giant bird. It looked like my days were numbered, but I was too numb to move. Hector and the ZARCs were probably driving the damn thing. I was surprised they hadn't landed right on top of me or sent a missile down my throat.

BLINK.

BETRAYAL

I blinked. My eyeballs were maybe freezing open. I saw some movement out of the helicopter door.

BLINK.

Stupid time had slowed down, for the dark figures were getting closer.

BLINK.

Now they were only a few feet away, with their machine guns out. I prepared my muscles for one last fling, intending to launch myself upward and take at least one of them to hell with me.

BLINK.

My stupid muscles wouldn't move. Wouldn't launch me. They rebelled. Instead I half rolled so that I ended up on my side, looking up at their fine military boots. Every second boot had a sheathed knife strapped to it.

BLINK.

The figures had parted, and a man was standing there in one of those gray parkas with fox fur. He pulled back his hood.

The face was familiar. Far too familiar. And I could not get a word out.

It was Dermot. Stupid, hairy Dermot.

A sight for sore, frozen eyes.

"Don't move, Amber. We have you. We have you. You're safe."

Eight

ABOUT THAT THERE SURGICAL PROCEDURE

I COULDN'T SPEAK A DAMN WORD. I couldn't swear. My body was not even really breathing. They lifted me and my double onto stretchers and brought us back to the helicopter, laying us on the floor. They slid silver sleeping bags around us, and like a nurse, Dermot began adjusting dials on the bags. They were perhaps the latest in electric vampire defrosting. I felt like a TV dinner.

"These will warm you up slowly," he said. "And I can keep track of your vital signs." He looked at his watch—an Apple Watch-like device. "There. Heartbeat slow but steady. I think you'll make it."

My throat was still too ragged to speak properly, but I spit out a few words. "What the hell...?"

And a few moments later I finished: "...are you doing here?"

"I'm happy to see you too," Dermot said. And despite myself, I *was* pleased to see him. Though I was so frozen I couldn't really say I was feeling much at all. The blanket was embracing me with a trickle of warmth.

I couldn't complete another thought. I slept. Woke to see Dermot still looking down on me. He was one of those humans I'd actually spent quality time with. We had a history, as they say. And he still had that somewhat cute, befuddled look about him. There even appeared to be empathy in his eyes.

I turned to discover my twin was still asleep.

Just that action seemed to tire me. So I conked out again. The next time I woke up they were carrying us off the helicopter. Cold hit my face but, thankfully, not the rest of me. The special ops were relatively gentle, and they carried us through a door that made me think we were on a ship. Then we went down a series of hallways and were, finally, placed in a sick bay. A male nurse in blue and gray fatigues with *US NAVY* across the pocket was waiting for us.

"How did you find me?" I asked.

Dermot waved the nurse away. "You don't want to know, Amber."

A dim alarm bell dinged in the back of my head. Anytime someone says, "You don't want to know," you really, really want to know. It's something my mom would've said.

"I do want to know," I said.

"Remember when you had that little blackout at the League's main base? When you hadn't fed?"

I remembered it well. I'd been put in a "sunshine" room with my meal in the next room. But they didn't provide me with proper documents to prove she was a moral kill. And after I ate her, I passed out, only to awaken in one of the League's medical rooms. They had been poking around at my interior, taking "samples."

"Yes, I remember," is all I said.

"And they, the League, that is—my League—they may have implanted a tracker in you while you were unconscious."

"*May have*? You sound like you didn't know anything about it. And that you're not sure."

"They did implant a tracker. And I had nothing to do with it, Amber. Scout's honor." He was smart enough not to put his hand over his chest.

"What! You expect me to believe that? You were near the top of the chain of command."

"I'd lost clearance from your files. They thought I'd been emotionally compromised. Both with you and Hallgerdur."

Well, they were right about that second one—his old murderous girlfriend. "And you stuck something in me. A tracker?"

"*They* did. It wasn't that big."

"As if size matters in this case. Well, I guess it does. But it's also the intention that counts. Where is it?"

"Your left buttock."

I nearly screamed. Someone had poked around in my cheek. Like, like some mad reverse buttock surgery.

"I can see you're getting a little angry," he said. He looked at his watch. At first I thought he was checking the time,

BETRAYAL

but he was reading my stats. "Heartbeat is up. Adrenaline up. It's totally understandable."

"I'm a little more than mad. Where is Chairman Margaret? I'd really, really like to give her a piece of my mind."

"She's dead."

My brain was still frozen. It took a moment for the words to sink in. "Dead?"

"Yes. There was…well, a cleaning out. Of the whole upper chain of command. Of all the bunker, in fact. And several other safe houses."

"A cleaning out? What do you mean?"

"The League was dismantled by an exterior force."

If I'd had the strength, I would have slapped him. "Stop using euphemisms! Tell it to me straight!"

"One of our enemies discovered our locations and sent strike teams to several of them at once. Nearly every person you met is dead. If there is still a League, then I and a handful of others are the last of the organization. It took all my contacts to pull off this mission."

"Who—who hit the League?"

"No solid information on that. But it is most likely ZARC Industries."

"They can do that? I mean, you were on American soil. How did they get there?"

"That's the thing about secret ops. They're so secret."

I didn't have it in me to laugh. In fact, I had very little in me at all. "So are you the one who phoned me a few hours ago? To warn me away?"

"Yes. We'd been looking for the base. Once we saw you moving in that direction, we knew you'd discover it. How did you do that?"

"I have library skills," I said.

"Yes. Well, you do have skills. Anyway, it became obvious what your destination was. My guess was that you were searching for your mother. I put two and two together."

"You must be so proud. So you tracked me anyway. Even if you didn't approve of the implant, you used it to track me."

"I know it wasn't right. But you'd be dead right now if I hadn't."

I couldn't really argue with that. "If the League was hit in several locations, then what happened to my father?" I pictured the last time I'd seen him, in that black coffin-like device being loaded into a black SUV.

"We lost him."

"He's dead?" I wasn't certain how I felt about this. He was a vampiric asshole.

"No. That cell was hit too. His sleep chamber is gone. Along with him. And everyone who was looking after him is dead."

"So ZARC has my father? Again?"

"There were signs of a struggle. But, well, we don't have a forensics team anymore. And the site was burned out. So I don't know his exact location."

It was all becoming too much to handle. But I had one more burning question to ask him. I fought gravity to raise my finger and pointed at my double. "Who the hell is she?"

BETRAYAL

Dermot shook his head. "I honestly have no idea. Why don't you tell me how you found her?"

I did. In whispers. When I mentioned the woman with metal hands, he raised his eyebrows. But when I brought up Hector the murderous AI, Dermot's face went as pale as snow. I could tell he had a million questions to ask me.

But before he could ask me one of them, I was out again. Fully, totally gone.

Nine

SCRATCHING AN ITCH

THE NEXT TIME I OPENED MY EYES, I was alone. Well, not entirely alone. My newly acquired look-alike vampire was sleeping in her bed across the room from me. They had strapped her arms and legs in several places. Her flesh was ghostly pale, as if the ice from the Antarctic Ocean would never leave her.

Dermot was gone, and the lights were all low. Grogginess was still playing punch-drunk love with my consciousness. I could move my arms and legs, so I swung out of the bed and set them on the floor, then stumbled about two feet before having to lean against the wall. I guessed the blood wasn't all running to my brain yet. Another stumble followed, and I nearly lost my footing.

An epic journey later I opened the door to the tiny washroom and closed it with a quiet *cathunk*. There was a stainless-steel toilet, stainless-steel sink and stainless-steel toilet-paper holder (with toilet paper on it that was not stainless steel). Even the inside of the Navy bathrooms looked like they could withstand a siege. I guessed the admirals didn't want to be caught on the can. I was surprised there wasn't a gun rack above the toilet.

The mirror showed a rather pale face, which was normal, but I did look thinner. After a cursory count, I was pleased to discover that I hadn't lost a single finger or toe to the cold. My hair was a letdown though. All frazzled and mussed. Not even that sexy mussed look. It was more the *I haven't showered in weeks* look. I was surprised Dermot hadn't commented on it.

But I wasn't here for a beauty contest. I couldn't stand having that tracker in me one more second. So I explored my left butt cheek. No indentation. But on my right butt cheek, I did find just the slightest unfamiliar lump. It might be fat. But there was only one way to tell.

I did a bit of exploratory surgery with my razor-sharp fingernails. There was very little blood, and in about thirty seconds I was holding a woodtick-sized electronic device. It even had little pincers. I set it on the counter, expecting it to scurry away. I opened the mirror and found some antiseptic, which stung. Then I discovered a bandage, and soon enough I had medically treated my most delicate posterior. It would hurt to sit for the next few hours. But I heal fast, and if there were scars, they'd be tiny. Not a problem anyway. I don't wear thongs.

I examined my tracker, impressed by its lightness and durability. That little electronic creature had been sending a signal through me for at least six months now. It would be picked up by a satellite and relayed back to the League. They knew every visit I'd made to the library in Mexico City, to the dojo, to the local taco stand. That irked me mightily! I could just squish the thing, but then they would know immediately that I'd taken it out. My next thought was to drop it down the toilet, and it would be forever be *beep-beeping* at the bottom of the ocean. Instead I slipped it into my pocket, leaving its fate to a future decision. I then washed my face and hands with warm water and made my way back to bed.

My thoughts were getting clearer. There was nothing like poking around in your own flesh to wake you up. I sat down on my bed and was about to stretch out when it became clear that my senses and thoughts were not totally reliable.

The bed across the room was empty.

The straps had been cut. There wasn't a single sign of struggle. Or a single sign of her.

I got up and wandered over to the door. It was one of those rounded ship doors, and it was locked from the outside, so it hadn't been opened. I turned. There were portholes on the far wall. One had been swung open, and the ocean waited outside. But the window itself wasn't much bigger than my head. Frankly, if she could crawl out that hole, she was a boneless wonder of nature—even more boneless than most vampires.

I suddenly glanced up, then let out a breath when I saw she wasn't on the ceiling.

There was a large stainless-steel refrigerator. And a cupboard beside it. I opened the cupboard first. A whole lot of medical supplies. No room for her. Next, I opened the

BETRAYAL

fridge to discover more medical supplies and a can of Coke. The light was a little blinding. I closed the door.

There were dust bunnies in front of the fridge. Dust on a military ship! I'd seen enough movies to know that was a no-no. They beat people with bars of soap in a towel for those kinds of errors. Or at least that's what *Full Metal Jacket* taught me.

So I grabbed both sides of the fridge and pulled. It rolled out, and I spun it at the last moment.

She was clinging to the back of the fridge.

"Hi," I said.

"Why do you look like *me*?" she asked.

"Why do you look like me?" I queried.

"What's your name?" she asked.

"What's *your* name?" I answered. "And why don't you let go of the fridge?"

She did so and took a step away. She fidgeted with her hands, holding them up as if she was trying to decide whether to take a defensive pose. She could barely stand up.

"Let's start at the beginning," I said. "I'll go first. My name is Amber Fang, and I have no fucking idea why you look like me."

The swear word startled her. But I was certain I had caught a glimpse of a smile.

"I'm Patricia," she said. "But you can call me Patty. "

"What were you doing in that underground ZARC bunker?"

"I was in an underground bunker?" This was followed by: "What's ZARC?"

Hmmm. Interesting. "Well, Patty, let's start with this. Where is the last place you remember being conscious?"

"China. Beijing, to be specific. I was hunting there."

"Hunting what?"

"Humans," she said, giving me an odd look, as if I'd just asked a horrendously stupid question. "There's lots of game to hunt over there."

"Yes, well, and what happened?"

"Well, I was in a smartphone warehouse. It was shut down. But I had cornered what I thought was a lone worker. Then this woman popped down from the ceiling. She had metal hands. Hard metal hands."

This was starting to sound familiar.

"So they had set up a trap for you?"

"She was strong, and she had come with a team of men in red-and-black fatigues. And great big electric guns. Next thing you know, I was on the floor. And knocked out." She drew in a breath and looked around the room. "And now I'm here."

"You don't remember anything in between?"

"I had a dream I was swinging a big sword and cutting arms off an octopus. But that must be just a dream."

"Maybe." I remembered how she had come awake and saved my derriere. "You were caught by an international arms-dealing organization called ZARC. There were three of you that they were experimenting on."

"Experimenting?" She looked down at herself.

"I'm only guessing. They had you in these electronic eggs."

"And what happened to the other two?" she asked.

"Dead," I said. I didn't like thinking of that. It was partly my fault. But I couldn't visualize how I could've

BETRAYAL

rescued them. And, of course, I'd had no idea that Hector existed.

She ran her hand through her hair. It was a similar color to mine. "Do you know who they were?"

I shook my head. "Now to the more pertinent point, as to why we look alike."

"It is odd. I feel as if I am talking to myself."

"I've been having the same experience." And it was true. I implicitly trusted her, though was that just because her face looked so much like mine? A sisterly bond. "What was your mother's name?"

"Tabitha," she said.

Well, that was no help. Mom's name is Nigella. Plus, it was impossible that Patty was one of my mom's offspring. I am the only one. I am pretty certain I'd have memories of a sibling. Patty also seemed younger than me, though we vampires do age rather gracefully. Humans would kill for that gene.

In fact, maybe they were.

"And who was your father?" I asked.

"Martin Horsus," she said.

My gut did a gut flip. "My father was named Martin too," I said. Even his name caused me to spit up a bit of revulsion. I swallowed. Then my second realization. Mom had kept her own last name. She was a vampire feminist. The best type. "Was Dad a bit of a dick?" I asked.

"I haven't seen him for a long time," she said. "I barely remember him from when I was a kid. But yes, he was a dick. Mom didn't like him much."

ARTHUR SLADE

She was my half sister. I was standing in front of my damn half sister. A family member I never ever dreamed I had.

"You're my half sister," I said.

Her eyes were as gray as mine. I wanted to reach out and hug her. I didn't know that I'd ever had that feeling, other than with Mom. And maybe once with Dermot, but I was vulnerable.

"I don't believe it," she said. She put her hand to my face. "I just don't believe it. But here you are."

And suddenly I did hug her. It...it felt like home. Melodramatic home.

"I should come clean," my sister said. "About something."

"About what?" I pulled back.

"Well, Tabitha, my mom. She was my father's sister."

"Dad slept with his sister!"

"No! No!" She put up her hands. "No. She wasn't really my mom. She just raised me. I never knew my real mom. I... well...I was told I was an orphan. But now I think maybe Mom didn't really die."

My brain slowly put two and two together. "You think my mom is your mom?"

She nodded.

Mind. Totally. Blown.

This meant Mom had had a child before having me and leaving the land of vampires to travel all around the world. Patricia was my older sister.

Damn her! She looked younger than me.

Ten

FACTIONS, PODS AND COUNCILS

THERE'S A WORD FOR WHEN you first meet a previously unknown relative who looks just like you.

Gobsmacked!

She was just so damn familiar. She stood in front of me, scratching at the side of her neck, a mannerism of my own and my mom's. Although the more I looked at Patty, the more I saw the few differences. Her nose was slightly upturned, in a shape that was a bit more like Dad's. Her hair was a lighter shade, with a few blond highlights—though those could have been added.

There were so many things I wanted to ask her. What music did she listen to? Who was her favorite novelist? Or did she even like books?

"You keep staring at me," she said.

"I can't help it. It's so damn eerie. I don't meet many vampires. Especially not ones who are family. Actually, come to think of it, most of the ones I meet are family. How many vampires are there? Where do you live? Who's your favorite novelist?"

ARTHUR SLADE

"Whoa!" She put up her hands. "Not so fast. I have no idea how many vampires there are. The Grand Council doesn't let little vamps like me know that stuff. We all have our own pods."

"Pods?"

"Family groups. I think they used to be called clans, but *pods* sounds so much more modern. We lived in Texas, though we moved around. The Fangs, Horsuses, Megraldas, Bakras—we were all one pod. Sometimes several pods get together. I don't like all the politics."

There was one burning question. It had been rattling around in the back of my head for a few minutes now. But I didn't want to spit it out. Yet spit it out I did: "And how do you hunt?"

"Hunt? Carefully. Why?"

"I mean, are there rules around hunting? Who do you choose to eat?"

"Well, I find kids don't have enough blood for a full meal."

"What!" I jerked away from her.

"I'm kidding, sis. Kidding. Oh, and now I've made a pun. I'm sorry on both accounts. But rules? Why would you ask that? Vampires are at the top of the food chain. We don't need feeding rules. Just don't kill too many humans in one area. And try not to take anyone too popular—like famous people."

I was getting chills. "So any human can be food?"

"That's the official line. Look, Amber, I know we just met. And I feel I can trust you, but..."

"But...?"

BETRAYAL

"The Grand Council executes sympathizers."

"Remind me what a sympathizer is."

"Someone who has a moral conscience about dining on humans. Who…well, for instance, only dines on murderers. Where have you been living? Why would you ask questions like this?"

"I've been on my own," I said, trying not to sound too whiny. "For a long time now."

"They kill lone wolves too."

Who *didn't* want to kill me these days?

She scratched at her neck again. "I've seen it—a sympathizer bound and gagged on a table. And everyone is supposed to take a bite."

"Everyone?"

She turned a little paler and stared down at the floor. "Every single vampire. They even check your teeth to be sure you're blooded."

Maybe it wasn't so bad that I'd spent my formative years with one motherly vampire. "We have to live in the human world," I said.

"Yes. I…I have a feeling we have similar tastes in food," Patty said. "Our pod only targets those who deserve death. I mean, every branch of the pod is different."

"So you only hunt murderers?"

"Yes. But where I come from, you have to be secretive about it. I, for instance, only hunt humans who have killed other humans. Gang members, human traffickers. All easily explainable deaths."

It made sense. And it was easier than my mother's *they must not have felt remorse* addendum.

"We are sisters at heart," she said. She whispered that last word and put her hand on mine. "I'm so glad you found me." I could feel her heartbeat pulse. Our hearts were beating at the same time.

The door clunked open. Dermot bumbled in. Perfect Dermot timing!

Patty leaped straight up to the ceiling, crawled like a spider at super speed across it and popped down in front of Dermot. It was an amazing display. My mouth dropped open in awe.

"Der—" I began.

Smack! She punched him in the face.

"—mot," I finished.

Smack! She cracked him in the face again.

He did manage to get a hand up to block the third blow, but his nose was already bleeding. Maybe even broken.

"Wait, Patty!" I said. "He's a friend!"

But she didn't stop. And he either was holding back his augmented moves, or she was that much faster, because every second blow landed.

"Patricia!" I shouted. I sounded like my mom. "Stop it! He's a friend. Don't wreck his face." I don't know why I shouted out that last part.

She pinned his arms to one side and went for a bite, teeth flashing. "Don't eat him!" I dashed over without using the cool ceiling-crawling trick. I'd have to get her to teach me how to do that. I grabbed her arm and yanked her back, and

BETRAYAL

she slashed toward me. Her eyes were bat-shit wild. Like she was ready to tear out my throat.

"Calm down!" I shouted and gave her a shove. She smashed into the bed, breaking the bolts that held it to the floor, then jumped back up to her feet. It dawned on me that yelling probably wasn't the best thing to do. "Calm down," I said more quietly, as I did my best to become a vampire whisperer. "He's not the enemy. He won't hurt you, Patricia. It's me. It's your sister. Calm down."

Her eyes cooled. Then warmed. By that, I mean she didn't look like she was going to tear my throat out. "Sorry," she said. "I haven't eaten in a while."

"Are you okay, Dermot?" I asked. I glanced over my shoulder.

"Sister?" The confused look on his face was priceless. He dabbed at his nose and came back with blood. "Why am I not surprised?"

"She's just a little touchy," I said. "She's been trapped in a tin can for—wait, what's the last date you remember?"

"October sixteenth," she said. "That's when I was in Beijing."

"It's March fifteenth. You've been out for five months."

"That explains the hunger." She put her hand on her stomach. "What's your friend's name again?"

"I'm Dermot," he said. "I'm pleased to meet you." He put out his hand, and she stared at it for a moment like she'd bite it. Then she shook it. He continued to hold his nose with his other hand.

"I'm Patricia Horsus," she said. "I'm sorry about what I did to your face."

ARTHUR SLADE

"I'll heal. Besides, your sister has done worse."

"It is a pretty face," Patty said.

Dermot blushed. He actually blushed. Anger and a pinch of jealousy rose up in me like a twin-headed Loch Ness Monster.

"Enough about faces," I said. "Dermot is a friend. He… he saved us from that island. We would have frozen to death."

"Are you military, Dermot?" she asked. "Navy? I don't see a uniform."

"That's classified," he answered.

"Oh," I said. "You'll find him a bit of a stickler for rules. It's a little frustrating."

"There are reasons for rules," Dermot said, channeling his inner schoolmarm. "Next time, I won't come in unannounced. Or without protection."

"Oh, you won't need protection with me," my sister said in a svelte voice. Dermot ignored the subtext.

"We are close to docking," he said.

"Where are we?" Patty asked, perhaps a little too quickly. "Or is that classified too?"

"Mare Harbour," Dermot said. "In the Falkland Islands."

"Ah, a United Kingdom territory," Patty said.

I was impressed. She at least knew her geography and had some geopolitical awareness. "Technically, they have their own legislature," Dermot corrected, "but yes, they are friends with Britain. And we are friends with Britain, so we can dock here without causing a fuss."

"And will we be getting out of here?" Patty asked, pointing to me and then herself. "I have been asleep for more than fifty winks. I have friends and family who might be missing me. Oh, and I need to update my Facebook status."

"I want to be sure you're medically sound," Dermot said. He really did have all the finesse of an accountant. "It's best for your health."

"How long will it take to do those tests?" Patty asked.

"It shouldn't be long at all."

She looked over at me, one eyebrow raised. "Is he always this evasive?"

"Just ask him about his love life. You'll find out."

She nodded. "Will you be doing the inspections?"

"No." It looked like he was going to blush again.

"Now, sis," I said, "he leaves the medical work to others. Just be sure to check yourself for trackers."

That got a partial blush out of him.

"Well, I have plenty of patience," Patty said. "And I do appreciate your diligence. I assume you'll be bringing me food."

"We will solve that problem," Dermot said. "One way or another."

I thought back to the last time they'd solved that problem for me. Locking a meal in the room next door. She'd been a serial killer. At least, I was pretty certain she was. I still hadn't seen the paperwork.

"Well, I'll sit tight until then," Patty said. "I'm putting myself entirely in your hands. At least the scenery is pleasing."

She was looking directly at Dermot. And this time he completely blushed.

Eleven
SISTERLY TALK

"ARE YOU ALWAYS SUCH A FLIRT?" I asked after Dermot left. I assumed he was flossing his teeth, primping his hair and freshening his breath at this moment. Oh, and setting his nose. I'd been gripping the foam pillow on my bed a little too hard. There were gouges in it.

"Humans are hilarious. Their blush reflex is so easy to trigger. And it makes me hungry." She licked her lips. They were very much like my lips. "Doesn't it make you hungry too?"

"No."

"But he makes you hungry?"

"No!"

She patted me on the shoulder, then gave it an affectionate squeeze. "Ah, Amber, you've been living on your own too long. It's obvious you have a thing for this man. Sad, but obvious. Humans are so weak."

"He's not weak." My traitorous voice actually squeaked as I said this. "He's been augmented."

BETRAYAL

"I bet he has!" She gave me two thumbs-up. "That reminds me, have you ever had sex with a man, then ate him?"

"What? No! And the proper tense is *eaten*."

"Thanks for the grammar check, sis." She sat on her bed. "Anyway, men really enjoy the first part. Not so into the second part. But they taste better. And boy, do their eyes ever get wide after that first bite."

"What the hell are you talking about?" I was strangling my pillow by this point.

Patty rolled her eyes. "I'm kidding, sis. Totally kidding. Mom—I mean, Aunt Tabitha—she thought my sense of humor was just a little over the top. Too macabre even for vampires."

I took a few deep breaths, somewhat surprised at the tension I was feeling. I exhaled. "It takes some getting used to."

"Well, we still have lots to learn about each other. And plenty of time to do it in too."

"I know. Do you ever get time to read? Who are you reading these days?"

"Are you a teacher or something?"

"A librarian."

She wrinkled up her nose like someone had passed chlorine gas. "I see. I don't read books. I'm more into Netflix." She looked around the room as though sizing it up. "Do you really think he'll let us go?"

"Us?"

She pointed at the door. "Well, he did lock the door when he went out."

ARTHUR SLADE

"I'm sure I can leave whenever I want. Dermot likely doesn't want an unknown vampire stalking around his battleship."

"Military men can be so sensitive that way. So do you think he'll let me go?"

"Yes," I said, though not with a lot of force.

"Oh, that sounded hesitant."

"Well, his organization has been struck hard by an outside force." Gee, I was talking like him now. "I think he's reorganizing things. It may take a little bit longer before he lets you out."

"So the League has been hit? Interesting."

"You know about the League? And that he's part of it?"

She shrugged. "I hear things. There was a rumor that they were hunting vampires."

"Yeah, they were. They hunted me."

"The vampires I heard about didn't come back." She hesitated, and I wondered if one of the vampires she was referring to was someone she knew. "So…who hit the League?"

"He didn't know. They have a long list of enemies, I imagine."

"Well, things are certainly shifting," Patty said. "The game is changing." She looked at me. "Are you part of the League?"

"No. No. Not now."

"But you were?"

"Let's just say I did some contract work for them."

"Well, that's vague enough." She gestured at our surroundings. "It must have been a good contract if they came all the way to Antarctica to rescue you."

BETRAYAL

"Yes. I guess it was." I didn't want to mention the bug in my butt. She already seemed to not trust them. Well, with good reason. I shouldn't trust them—but Dermot, he was a different story. If I looked in my little heart of hearts, I did trust him.

"What were you doing in Antarctica anyway?" she asked.

"Oh, it's a very long story."

Patty yawned. "I get it." Then, quite suddenly, she jumped toward me. I put up my hands, but she knocked them aside.

And hugged me. Tightly. The smell of her hair. The contact. It was what family members did all the time. "I am so, so, so pleased to find you," she said. "I've often felt like there was something missing from my life. Some connection. And here you are."

"Yes. Me too." Well, actually, I hadn't thought very often about siblings. Only because Mom hadn't mentioned any. Then again, I did have the typical only-child fantasies. "I always wanted an older sister."

She kissed my cheek. "Well, sleep well, sister. I really, really am happy. In this very moment. I'll cherish it forever, Amber."

"I'll cherish it too. Now have a good sleep. We'll have plenty of time to talk tomorrow. I'll start at the very beginning and tell you everything."

I went to my bed and she to hers. I was completely asleep within a few heartbeats.

Despite my happy mood, my dreams were unintelligible and dark. An array of leering shadows floated through my head. Then came a *thunk* sound. It made me think of a car crash. That became part of the dream. But another *thunk* grew more insistent. It meant something. Stirred my thoughts to waking.

I opened groggy eyes. Wiped them. Turned my head.

The door was open. By *open* I mean nearly torn off. And Patty was no longer in her bed.

A jet of adrenaline got me to slide my legs over the side of the bed and onto the floor. She had pulled the door from its hinges. I didn't know if I would have had the strength to do that. The guard was on the floor, his head at an odd angle, his face bruised. I jumped over and put my hand on his neck and felt for a pulse. Still alive.

She had left me. Abandoned ship. There was a set of stairs that clearly led to the upper deck. I took two steps that way, certain she had fled the battleship, but turned purely on instinct and looked down the hall that led deeper into the ship. There was another marine on the floor there. Why on earth would she go that way?

When I got up to the marine, I saw my sister hadn't been so kind to him. Judging by the blood on his forehead, this man's skull had met something metal. He would not be waking up anytime soon. In fact, he might never wake up at all.

The metal floors were easy to walk or even run quietly on in bare feet. I sped down the hallway and up another set of stairs, passing two unconscious sailors. Then I turned a corner and lost my footing as I slid through guck and some sort of liquid. I skidded against the wall and held myself up.

BETRAYAL

The guck was blood. There was a marine's body on the floor in front of me, but his head was partway down the hall. I was standing in an ever-widening and congealing pool of his blood.

It was obvious she hadn't fed on him. Patty had killed, not to eat and not in self-defense. Only a part of my brain was assimilating that information. My feet were painted red. Oh, gross! I continued down the hall. She was a lot easier to track now because she'd left bloody footprints. She had gone up to a door, stopped, then up to the next door, and then the prints went dry. It was clear she was hunting for something. Or someone.

Then I stopped. Silence. No, the thud of a heartbeat. Then two hearts. Two hearts beating. One was beating slow. The other had a normal beat.

I shoved the nearest door open. The cot in the corner was empty, along with the rest of the room. It looked fancy enough though. Maybe the captain's wife stayed here.

Across the hall I heard a sigh. A familiar gurgle. It almost sounded sexual.

I hopped across to the door and twisted the handle. Locked. I pushed then with a feminine but Hulkish effort, shoving the door open.

My sister was in the room, straddling Dermot's half-naked body.

They were having sex! A volcano of anger erupted in my brain. What the hell! Why would he sleep with my sister?

Then I saw he still had his pajama bottoms on and was clearly unconscious.

Patty was very busy feeding.

Twelve
BETRAYAL IS A BITCH

SHE TURNED HER HEAD the slightest bit sideways—not wanting to break the suction—and gave me a half wave that might have been apologetic. Dermot was doing his best impression of a pale coma patient. Clearly, her paralytic agent was working fine.

On the wall behind her were two military sabers and a rather mean-looking spear gun. I imagined Dermot was just using an officer's room as his own. But the weapons were too far away to be of any use to me.

So I leaped. An arrow of fury and flesh, zipping straight at her. Patty managed to duck enough to bring up one hand that guided me right into the wall face first. She did all this without losing an iota of suction, then shook her finger at me as I tried to pull myself to my feet, holding my head. Patty, of course, said nothing.

I eventually got to my unsteady feet. Two Pattys and two Dermots wavered before me. I pointed at the four of

BETRAYAL

them with all the gumption I could summon. "Get off him!" I shouted, but it came out, "Geff off hmmm!"

This got another finger shake from Patty. Two, technically, since I was still seeing double—the older sisters telling the younger sister she was being naughty. The two Dermots were turning paler by the second.

I blinked. Waited until there was only one finger pointing at me and then took another jump, landed a foot or so away, grabbed Patty and pulled. She held on to the bed, which was obviously bolted to the floor, and sucked and sucked. It was like pulling on a giant leech. I set my feet, and she tore through the mattress with her nails but remained clamped to Dermot. I gave an Amazonian pull, and she came loose from the bed, along with Dermot. He hit the floor first, she second.

She was still attached to his neck. Her suction must be legendary!

"Stop it! Stop it!" I dragged them half across the room, then changed tactics. I put one foot on Dermot's chest and grabbed Patty's hair and yanked. This time the suction broke with a *smurp* noise. I couldn't tell if he was still alive. His neck was a huge mess of red, and some blood was spurting out.

"I wasn't done!" Patty said, wiping her face. "Damn you, sis! Get your own meal!"

She punched me full in the solar plexus, which made me let go of her hair. Then she flipped up and launched herself toward me, slamming me backward against a wall. She twisted her hands around my neck in a choke hold.

"Don't eat my friends!" I said, while trying to pry her hands away.

"Humans can't be friends!" She quickly slipped behind me with her arm over my windpipe in a sleeper hold—aiming to close off my carotid artery and the blood flow to my brain. I'd seen it in the movies and had practiced counteracting it with my *sifu*. I pried off the hand that was pulling back my head, creating some separation that allowed me to elbow her in the guts. She lost her hold, and I spun to face her.

"He killed Dad!" she shouted. She obviously had some martial arts training, because she was kicking me in the face as she said this.

"No, he didn't!" I caught her leg and pulled her off-balance, attempting to throw her into the wall. She landed on both feet. "At least, I'm pretty sure he didn't. Dad's with ZARC now."

"Mom really got to you," she said. "She chose you! You! And left me there!"

It was true. And Mom had never once mentioned that I had a sister. Why?

I grabbed a saber off the wall, and Patty's eyes widened.

"Do you know how to use it?" she asked.

"Of course!" I'd never swung a sword. I assumed this one was best for poking a hole through her, not for chopping. Since it was ceremonial, the blade likely wasn't sharp.

Patty yanked the spear gun from the same wall, brought it up and pointed it at my chest. I froze. She was too far away for me to reach with my blade.

BETRAYAL

"Sorry, sis," she said. Then pulled the trigger.

Nothing happened. She pulled it again. And again. I went to give her a poke in the shoulder, but she parried with the gun, then ripped out the spear thingy and stuck me with the pointy end.

In the hand. She essentially stapled it to the wall. I screamed in pain and rage and pulled, but the damn thing wouldn't come out of the metal. I was stuck there in a half-religious pose.

"I'm sorry I killed Darren," Patty said.

"Dermot! His name is Dermot."

She raised a hand and took a moment to catch her breath. "Whatever. He did seem nice, for a human. Smelled nice too. But he was the last of the League. I've sworn to hunt them down since they caught Great-Grandma." She sucked another breath. At least I'd winded her.

It was too painful to try to unhook my hand from the wall. She'd jammed half the length of the spear into the wall. "You should run," she said in a conspiratorial whisper. "Away from here. I know you've been brainwashed by Mom, but you can't trust any of the humans. None of them at all. They'll never have your best interest at heart."

Then she dove for the porthole. Which was open and just wide enough for her head. She could do the double-jointed vampire-bone trick at speed, apparently, because with a smooth motion she made her shoulders fold together and slide through.

And she would have escaped, just like that, but she couldn't change the size of her backside. Her forward momentum came to a halt as her rear end got stuck. She became a cork in a bottle.

"You're too big in the heinie, sister," I shouted. I didn't know if she could hear me, because her butt was blocking the only way for sound to travel. But she wiggled from side to side, comically kicking her legs.

I laughed. Then I heaved myself toward her, pulling my hand to the end of the spear. It was painful, and there was blood. Lots of it. It is the worst sight in the world to see blood dripping out of my own body. But I got close enough to grab her right leg. She managed to blindly connect with a kick that knocked me back and pushed her ahead a few inches. She was going to get through!

I grabbed her leg again, but it was like wrestling with an anaconda with one hand. I still couldn't detach from the wall.

It was clear I would never be able to pull her back inside with just one hand. I cursed several times. Then my brain, my lovely brain, had a flash of inspiration. I reached into my pocket, found the tracker, drove my nail into the flesh of her posterior and then shoved the tracker into the wound. It clung there. Then it unclamped its little legs and climbed deeper.

"Whadahell!" Patty's muffled shout made its way into the ship.

Then, with a *ploop*, she worked her fanny through the window and dived downward. There was a splash a moment later.

I drew in a deep breath.

BETRAYAL

"Don't move!" A marine stood at the door. He was clutching a machine gun in his hand.

"I can explain all of this," I said. I tried to gesture with my right hand, but it was still stuck to the wall, and I was bleeding like a stuck pig. "Or maybe I can't."

"I'll explain part of it," Dermot said below me. His voice was a whisper, but loud enough for the marine to hear. "Turns out your sister isn't all that nice."

Thirteen

MR. McGRATH AND MR. HEXDALL

"YOU'RE ALIVE," I SAID.

Dermot didn't answer. That little quip was apparently all he had energy for before passing out again.

"Did you hear what he said?" I pointed at Dermot. "My sister did all of this. She's a real home wrecker."

Johnny marine didn't seem to care. "Don't move! Or I'll blow your head off."

I stood there, doing my best not to fall over, because the pain was really getting to me. Another marine showed up, then another, each equally gruff. They kept their guns trained on me.

"Easy boys," I said. "I'm on your side. Really, I am."

The first marine came closer, now that his brothers had the bead on me, and pried the spear from the wall. Gritting my teeth, I pulled it out of my hand and dropped it to the floor. The whole time, the square-jawed marines had their guns pointed at me. I leaned against the wall and did my best impression of

BETRAYAL

an Amber painting. I didn't want to do anything that would induce them to pull their triggers. All it would take was one nervous Nellie, and I'd be splattered across the wall.

Then more marine types charged in, pointing more guns, until it became rather ridiculous. I blinked, feeling I might pass out, but a deep breath steadied me. I was soon handcuffed, Dermot was loaded onto a stretcher, and we were both taken to the sick bay. Those guns continued to point at me.

My stupid hand kept bleeding. Kept aching. I wondered if there would be any permanent damage.

Dermot looked really pale. Thankfully, Patty hadn't finished feeding, or he'd be white as a sheet and dead as a goat. Of course, the last vampire who nearly sucked out every last drop of his blood was me. He might be the only human to be bitten by sister vampires. Maybe he could get a tattoo. Or a medical bracelet stating that fact.

The male nurse had wheeled in blood bags on a pole, and it wasn't long before tubes were snaking in and out of Dermot's neck and arms. I did worry he'd made the wrong career choice. He seemed prone to blood loss and medical distress. Once when his ex-girlfriend shot him, once when I sucked his blood, and now my sister. And those were only the incidents I knew of. Maybe he should have trained to be an accountant.

It could be I was his bad-luck charm—although you couldn't blame the Icelandic hitwoman, Hallgerdur, on me.

A woman in blue-and-gray fatigues charged into the room. She had the build of a boxer and eyes that looked to be made of slate. *DR. PARNUS* was written along one pocket. "Just step back, gentlemen. If she'd wanted to kill us, you all would have died in your sleep last night." When they didn't move, she added, "That's an order."

They stepped back and lowered their weapons, but not their eyes.

"And someone undo her cuffs," Parnus added.

This was done by a marine with sweat on his forehead.

Dr. Parnus spent a few minutes with Dermot, then came over to me. She took my good hand and guided me to a seat on a bed. "Jesus, no one's been brave enough to patch you up." She took a glance at my wound and gave me my first medical prognosis. "It's messy. But the spear missed any bones. In a month or two, it should be good to go."

"Happy to hear it," I said. I knew I'd heal much more quickly than that. She wiped the blood away with a cloth and spread some orange liquid on the wound, followed by a paste that I assumed was a topical anesthetic because my hand grew warm, then numb. She stuck a hypodermic into my wrist without asking.

"Tell me if this hurts." She was pulling out what looked like a sewing needle and fancy thread.

It didn't hurt. So I was pleased. It was like watching a documentary about stitching on TV. That's how well the local anesthetic was working.

"I don't suppose you could tell me what happened in there?" she asked as she tied up the last stitch on my hand.

BETRAYAL

"A bit of a sisterly quarrel," I said.

"It's more than a quarrel. Mr. McGrath is missing most of his blood."

"Who?" I said, somewhat dumbly.

She pointed at Dermot. "Mr. McGrath."

I suddenly realized I'd never heard his last name. All this time, and I didn't know even that detail about him. Why didn't he tell me?

Or why didn't I ask?

"He shouldn't be alive," the doctor added.

"That, honestly, I can't explain. I'll have to leave it to him. I'm not certain what's classified and what isn't. I do know he's tough. Dumb but tough."

I wondered if his augmentations had somehow saved him. Maybe he produced blood faster than the average human. When I was sucking his blood back in Iceland, I didn't experience any particularly strange taste. Of course, I was in a bit of a feeding frenzy then. I really wanted to look a bit more deeply into what exactly had been done to him.

"You should be bleeding more," she added. She pulled out a pair of scissors and cut off the ends of the stitches.

"I heal fast. I'm a walking miracle."

That was all I could come up with. I was just a little too tired, too betrayed, and feeling like an emotional punching bag. Things just kept happening to me. I really had to finish my Master of Library Science and find a nice quiet library to retire in. File me under *vacation*.

And I'd do that, I promised myself. Right after I found my mother. Oh, and killed my sister. Then I could disappear into the land of librarianship.

"Well, that should do it," Dr. Parnus said. "Usually I'd suggest leaving the stitches in for ten days, but it might be a shorter period with you. Come to me to get them removed."

"I'll be able to do it myself," I said. I flexed my fingers on my left hand, showing my sharp nails.

"I'm sure you can."

She went back over to Dermot. He still hadn't awakened, but at least he looked less pale.

I laid back. I was going to put my hands behind my head in a show of coolness, but the motion turned into sharp pain that forced me to grimace. I crossed my arms instead. I decided to enjoy my free thoughts before the freezing wore off.

Mom! Why the hell didn't you tell me about my sister?

When I thought of all the heart-to-hearts we'd had, not once had she even hinted that Patty existed. Any question about my father or aunts or family of any sort had led to her clamming up entirely. Or she'd give me some quip that deflected my question.

I had a sister!

And she'd left me. I mean, I got that part. She didn't trust humans. But the biting my boyfriend—

What? What was that? I hadn't meant to use that word. He was my work partner. My sometimes boss. Maybe even my friend.

And Patty had tried to eat him. That was beyond the pale—a humongous betrayal. She obviously didn't have much

BETRAYAL

use for humans, nor did she mind eating someone else's food—not that he was my food. But in America, if you tried to take a steak away from a cowboy, you'd soon be missing a few teeth.

A familiar face walked into the room. It was attached to a head, which was attached to the rest of the man's body. He was clad in a black suit like a character in *Men in Black*. The man was in his midforties and muscular, and he gave me a particularly hard glare, then walked over to Dermot and the doctor.

I'd hunted this man once. He had pretended to be a murderer, and I'd stalked him down an alley in Seattle, believing he was my next meal. But it had all been a ruse by the League in an attempt to capture me. Next thing I knew they were shooting darts at me, and I'd fled.

"Jordan Rex," I said as he approached.

"My real name is Michael Hexdall," he said. "You know that." He did not seem amused.

"Well, it's a pleasure to see you, Mikey."

"Likewise," he said without seeming to mean it. "What went on in here?"

"Well, Patty—my sister as it turns out—broke out of the room we were locked in, ran amok for a bit and then took a big bite out of Dermot. If I hadn't interrupted their little *tête-à-neck* he'd be dead right now."

"Well, we're lucky you were around, aren't we? And what became of your sister?"

"She jumped out the porthole. Well, first she got stuck because her butt is bigger than mine." I wasn't sure if that factoid was true. "But she managed to squirm away. Alas, she didn't share her travel plans with me." I kept the fact of the tracker to myself. "She was too busy stabbing me in the hand." I held up my damaged hand.

"The British navy is out looking for her now. Was she wounded?"

"Only her pride. I'm pretty sure I would've won against her. Really, I am. I am." Maybe the doctor had given me something that was spacing me out. Hexdall's head grew two sizes bigger, then shrunk down. Yep, something was in my bloodstream!

My hand was starting to burn with pain. The funny thing about having a quick-healing system is that any anesthetic wears off far too quickly.

"I'm sure you would have," Hexdall said without even trying to sound convincing. I bet he had voted against the whole *Let's go to Antarctica and save Amber* mission. "Well, heal well, Miss Fang. I may have a few questions for you, so please stick around."

I nodded toward the guards. "I don't think they'd let me go. They keep making eyes at me."

"Oh," he said, raising one finger. "Please make this mental note: I am immune to your attempts at humor."

Immune! But I was hilarious. I chuckled somewhat madly and searched hard for a witty comeback. And continued to search and search.

"Well, dammit," I whispered.

He looked at me as if I were insane. Then, without a backward glance, he walked out of the room.

BETRAYAL

Dr. Parnus was filling out charts at one end of the room. Marine boys were watching me like brush-cut hawks. So I did the only thing I could do. I lay back, closed my eyes and slept.

Fourteen

WHERE TO PUT A TRACKER 101

I WOKE UP IN THE BRIG. I must have slept hard and deep, because I had no memory of being carried out of the sick bay and placed in the cell. My new room was four feet by six feet, and there was no porthole, of course, and really not much going for it other than an open-air toilet and a sink. And one mattress. Which I was lying on. It looked as if they'd set up bars in a vacant corner of the ship. The military never did anything too fancy.

A marine stood about five feet away, one hand on his pistol. At least he didn't have it drawn and pointed at me. The door behind him was closed and, I assumed, also locked. There were some curious trust issues here, although I didn't blame anyone. My sister had just torn a metal door off its hinges. I'm sure that fact alone had freaked out their military think-boxes. And they couldn't help but wonder what I was capable of.

I was certain my sister was stronger than me. I've ripped the doors off houses and cars, but something that solid—well, that just seemed out of the realm of possibility. But it would be fun to try.

I sat up. The marine tightened his grip on his pistol handle and shuddered. Gee, they'd given me the jumpiest marine on the seven seas. I was glad he hadn't shot himself in the foot.

"Hey, sailor," I said. "Can a gal get a drink?"

"Th-there's a sink in your cell."

"I usually don't drink out of sinks. I'm looking for a splash of wine. Perhaps a merlot. I love the red stuff."

"Just drink out of the sink." He was a bit gruffer this time.

"Well, I'm a bit of a fancy gal. I like things clean, for one." Actually, that wasn't a fair complaint. The brig was spotless.

"I'm not coming near that cage. If you're feeling thirsty, drink from the sink. Those are my orders."

"Why so hostile toward me?" I asked.

"I lost two of my buddies last night." I realized two things at once. I felt sorry for him. And I hadn't slept the whole night. Only a couple of hours must have passed since my trip to sick bay. "Rumor is it was your sister," he continued. "Not sure how she did it. They were tough as nails. And yet here you are, still alive on our ship. So I'm sorry if you're too dainty to drink out of the sink."

"I'm sorry to hear about your fellow marines," I said. And I really did mean it. My sister didn't mind killing anyone who got in her way. That fact was still rattling around my own think-box.

"They were my brothers."

I got that. I did. Now that I had a sister, I felt a slight affinity for her. Well, then again, I figured I might punch her in the solar plexus next time I saw her. Or rip her head off. But still, she was my sister.

I drank from the sink, and a few sips made me feel a bit better. My hand was aching, but not so much that I couldn't ignore it. The itch of healing was already starting.

The door swung open, and Hexdall barged in and motioned to the marine, who changed position to the far wall. Hexdall gave me a passable smile and waited by the door.

"I'm wondering if—" I began.

Hexdall raised his hand. "Just wait," he gruffed.

I do not like being interrupted, but I bit my tongue.

There was a clumping sound coming down the hallway. *Womp. Womp. Womp.* It made me think someone was pounding posts into the metal floor. The *womping* came closer, and someone swore after a particularly loud *womp!*

Then Dermot walked into the room. Upright. Pale as marshmallows. He was not under his own steam though. A robotic pair of legs had been attached to his own legs, making him a few inches taller. Those same robotics ran up his spine and along his arms. I'd seen exoskeletons in science fiction movies, but here was one in the flesh, so to speak.

"Good morning, Amber," he said. Despite his steam-train-loud arrival, his voice was not much more than a whisper.

"Good morning," I said. "How are you?"

"I'm operating at about 30 percent right now." He blinked slowly. Yep, he was not all there. "Open the cage." He gestured and obviously didn't have full control, because his metal fist banged into the wall and dented it.

"Are you certain, sir?" the marine said.

"Don't make me repeat myself."

The cage was opened—with keys, no less. They liked doing things old style here. The marine backed away as if he were facing down a rattlesnake.

"Thank you for saving me," Dermot said. He said it loud enough for the others to hear.

"You're welcome. Patty really hadn't asked my permission to eat you. Plus, you've had enough bites in your life."

He managed to put a hand to his neck without harming himself. "I'm pleased she was interrupted. I assume that means her feeding clock hasn't been reset, and she'll go into the same freezing frenzy that came over you."

That is one of the drawbacks of being a vampire. You have to slurp your meal until the food is dead. A chemical released at that moment resets the vampire feeding clock to about thirty days. If you don't finish your meal, eventually a switch in your head flips, and you go on an uncontrollable blood hunt until you're fed.

"I had been thinking along the same lines," I said. "The difference is, she probably doesn't care if she goes on a feeding frenzy. She's not as worried about eating the innocent as I am. And it might be kind of fun for her to let loose that way."

"Don't go getting any ideas," Hexdall said.

Dermot put up his hand, gears whirring, to stop my retort. "She is gone. That much we know for certain. This is a small island, so if she swam to shore, we'll find her. And Argentina is too far of a swim. She has information about how weak the

League is now. That might make things even more dangerous for us. It's a shame she got away."

"Umm...we haven't totally lost her," I said.

"Oh, can you track her with sisterly ESP?" Hexdall asked. Well, that was a poor attempt at humor.

"No. I pulled my tracker out of my butt, the one you guys stuck in me, and stuck it in her...um...upper leg."

"You did that all at once?" Dermot asked.

"No. I'd taken the tracker out on my own a few hours earlier and didn't want to throw it away, so I kept it in my pocket. Then I attached it to her just before she dove into the Atlantic. I'm pretty certain it stuck there."

"You're brilliant!" Dermot said. He swung the arm like he was going to pat my back, but it smashed into the wall again, missing Hexdall by an inch or so. "Jesus, these things are touchy. Sorry, Mike." Dermot managed a smile. "Well, we'd better get to tracking her."

He turned, and Hexdall followed him. The marine looked at me. No one had given either of us orders. "Well, I guess I'll just march on after them," I said.

He nodded. I stopped at the door and said, "I am sorry about your friends. Truly, I am. If it's any consolation, I'll make her pay for that."

"I'd prefer to do it myself," he said.

I left the brig.

Fifteen

EYES ON THE GREEN DOT

I THOUGHT I'D BE TAKEN to some secret situation room that would have trackers and all the high-tech screens I was used to seeing in Tom Cruise movies. But instead we were back in Dermot's room—me, him and Grouchface Hexdall. Someone had cleaned the blood off the floor and even hung a picture of a whale, so you couldn't see the hole the spear had poked in the wall.

Dermot pressed several buttons, and his exoskeleton opened up like a rib cage. He stepped out somewhat shakily and sat on the bed. He looked like he was about to faint, and I prepared to catch him. He teetered but didn't totter over. He did lean against his headboard though.

"You sure you should be on duty?" I asked. "You're looking a little pale."

"There's far too much to do, Amber," he said. "So many things are falling into line. And falling out of place. Plus, your sister could be far, far away by now. Or clinging to the hull of the boat."

"Just don't be a hero," I said. A glimmer of a smile appeared on his face.

Hexdall brought a black suitcase over and flipped it open. There was a smartphone inside, not a brand I recognized—perhaps it was a special kind only spy kids get to use. He attached something to the bottom of it and pressed a button, and it made an electronic *bong* sound.

"Well," Dermot said, "if the tracker attached itself properly to Patricia, we should be able to see where she is."

He *beep-bopped* on the phone, eventually settling on an app. I moved a little closer. He smelled of antiseptic mixed with a touch of Brut—had anyone used that aftershave since the 1980s? I sometimes wondered if the whole League had been transported to the present day in some sort of hot-tub time machine. At least they didn't have mullets.

Hexdall leaned like a leaning tower of grumpiness.

The phone had a large display, and it was showing us a map of the world. Dermot punched in a few numbers. There was a long pause, and I thought perhaps the screen had frozen.

Then a flashing red dot appeared on the map, and the app zoomed in automatically to the Falkland Islands—right to the dock we were docked at. Well, not in full definition, of course. But it looked like it was where I assumed the ship would be. "She is attached to the hull!" I said. Maybe she'd bashed her brain in on the way down.

"No. That's us. I have to hit the perambulator locator."

"Is that its real name?" I asked.

"No, but I know full well what you think of our inability to properly use technology. I just have to click the Find button. And *voilà*."

He did click a little owl symbol, and a green flash appeared.

"Oh my," Dermot drawled. "That's almost impossible."

The green dot was flashing above Venezuela—more than twelve hundred miles away—and it was clearly moving northward.

"She's made it to the mainland," Dermot said. "And is taking a flight north."

"She moves fast," Hexdall said. "She's obviously smarter than her sister."

I was going to argue with him, but he seemed to be right. I had no idea how Patty had gotten that far with such speed.

"How long has it been?" I asked.

Dermot looked at his watch. He might be the last human being on earth who still wears a windup watch. "Just under twelve hours. Somehow she made the three hundred miles to the mainland. Then caught a flight. A rather complicated thing to do, since she left here without any sort of identification or money."

The green dot continued to *blip, blip* its way northward.

Hexdall was looking at his own phone. He'd been using his meaty fingers to search Argentinian news sources. "Well, there is one fisherman who didn't come home last night. That would give her time, assuming a full gas tank, to get to the mainland in eight hours."

Had she killed some poor fisherman?

"Likely dead," Dermot said as if he were reading my mind. "So that would give her four hours to find a flight."

"Carjacking is my best guess," Hexdall said.

"Makes sense," Dermot agreed. "And it would be a woman, of course."

"Why?" I asked. I'd leaned against the headboard to get a better look. "She wouldn't be afraid of any man. She could take on three, I bet."

"She stole her identity." The way Hexdall said it made me think he really wanted to add *stupid* to the end of that sentence.

"So that gets her on the plane," Dermot said. "Someone will be missing, but the authorities probably wouldn't begin to search for a missing person until at least twelve hours have passed."

"Patty could go anywhere in the world," I said. "If she has enough cash."

"Yes, she could," Dermot said. "We'd better start following her now."

I looked at his pale face and saw that he had a bit of palsy. "You aren't going anywhere," I said. "Even with your fancy exoskeleton."

"You're right," he said quietly. "But that means you'll have to pursue her."

"I would love to. I have unfinished business with her. I'll need a ticket."

"I'll get two tickets. One for you and one for Hexdall."

You could hear my mouth drop open.

Sixteen

NO CONSOLATION PRIZE

"NO WAY IN HELL!" I shouted.

"It's the only way," Dermot said. He found the strength to tighten his jaw muscles. "I can't go. And I can't, in good conscience, send you alone."

"I'm a loner. I don't work well with assholes."

"Hexdall is not an asshole," Dermot said. It didn't sound convincing.

"Why, thank you, sir," Hexdall said. "I appreciate the vote of non-assholeness."

"And second," Dermot continued, "you are not a member of the League, Amber."

"Make me into one." Wait, what was I saying? Did I really want to work for them again? Of course, all that seemed to remain of the League was Dermot and Hexdall.

"I can't just do that. I don't have any of the forms with me. And frankly, the best I can do is make you an associate until we find out if there are any other members of the upper hierarchy left."

"I won't go with him. I don't want to." I knew I sounded petulant, and I also knew I was lying. I was dying to take another crack at my sister. Either in battle or to sit down and pick her brain. With an ice pick, if necessary.

"You will go, Amber," Dermot said, and the confidence in his voice was aggravating. "I know you. But you are wounded, so you need a partner. And I can't send League equipment without a proper agent to care for it." He pointed at the suitcase. "Nor can I use League funds without a sanctioned agent involved. There's too much paperwork."

Paperwork! The man was insane. His League had dipped down to two members, and he was still worried about paperwork.

"If it's any consolation," Hexdall said, "I don't really want to work with you either." His eyes glittered with humor. He was getting far too much of a kick out of all this. I was tempted to give him a literal kick to the solar plexus.

"As long as we're clear about that," I said. I slumped my shoulders. "Fine. I'll go. But on the plane I want to sit in a different row."

"I second that," Hexdall said.

"Good, good." Dermot patted my shoulder. His hand was cold.

"What about ZARC?" I said.

"What about them?" Dermot asked. "We're not really in a position to strike out at them."

"Well, I just want to remind you there's a murderous AI called Hector who, I assume, just downloaded himself somewhere else."

"They are that advanced with artificial intelligence?" Hexdall asked. "My last reports said they had to scrap that tech. It kept going insane."

"Well, it sounded insane to me. But still functional enough to try to take my life. It killed two other vampires right in front of me."

"Yes, I have been thinking about that," Dermot said. "It does mean they will be able to put together probability algorithms at great speed. Any actions of ours will be predicted. I just hope they didn't get enough information about you while you were in their bunker. There's nothing we can do about it now though."

"And what about my mother?"

"You did find your sister," Hexdall said. "That's like a near miss."

I shot him a glance that would wither a toad.

"Let's just say our resources are spread kind of thin, and I have other things on my plate," Dermot said. "We will get to your mother later. We have to follow this lead while it's live. Your sister might discover the tracker at any moment."

"But what do we do with her once we find her?"

He pointed his thumb toward his partner. "Hexdall is our expert vampire capturer."

"Has he ever caught one? Or do you only have the failed attempt on me to go by?"

"I have a 50 percent success rate," Hexdall said. He sounded proud of that figure. "We will figure out what to do once we catch up with her. I'm good at adjusting to the moment."

ARTHUR SLADE

"I'm going to need to eat. Soon." I counted on my fingers. "In about six days, to be exact. I do have a meal waiting in Mexico."

"I'll consider that," Dermot said. "I can't do anything until we know where Patty is going. But I'll add it to my list of things to do." He pretended to write it down. "*Find a moral meal for Amber. Check.*" I rolled my eyes at his sense of humor. "You have to go now. The helicopter leaves in fifteen minutes. I suggest taking a shower, Amber. Then get on your way."

I should have been insulted. But I did need a shower, if just to get the blood off me from the several battles I'd had in less than a day. A marine led me to another room with a private shower. I got cleaned up, leaving my hand out of the shower so as not to get the dressing wet. It hurt, and maybe that was one source of my anger. And yet I already felt, underneath that pain, the itch of regeneration. I've had a few bullet holes in my body—the worst being one in my leg that took a week to heal after I pulled the bullet out myself. Mom taught me how to do self-surgery when I turned twelve. It sounds like fun. But it's very much not. Especially when you don't have anesthetic.

When I stepped out of the shower, I found there were several pairs of pants and some shirts laid out for me. Even a pair of running shoes. Either Dermot, in his exoskeleton, had dropped them there or one of the marines had. Where he'd found the clothes, I didn't know. But it was good to dress in something fresh and new. One thing about the military is they keep clothes clean. I suddenly smelled lemony. I also

BETRAYAL

discovered a backpack with more clothing, a brush and even lipstick that was close to my color.

There was a knock on the door. I opened it to find Dermot waiting. He was back in his exoskeleton. "Departure in three minutes," he said. Hexdall stood behind him.

Dermot walked us up a set of stairs. He looked slightly less pale, though it may have been because it was a bit darker here. A marine opened a door, and we stepped into a windy day and walked toward a Navy search helicopter.

"How long are you going to be in that outfit?" I asked.

"Only a few days," Dermot replied. "It's not the most intuitive thing to operate." As if to prove this, he absentmindedly reached to scratch his head and punched himself instead. Not hard. But enough to make a small *smack*. "I can't wait to get out of it."

I rubbed his head where he'd hit it. "You better take care of yourself, Dermot. And don't poke out your eyes."

"It's you who should take care. Patty is, well, she's something else." He sounded almost impressed, and I'd admit to feeling a pinch of jealousy. "I don't know if she's faster. But she's certainly meaner. You may have to eliminate her."

"My sister?"

"She killed two men on this ship. Two more, most likely, in her escape. I'm just preparing you for all the options."

"I'm prepared."

"I'll be keeping in touch as you travel. I do wish I could go with you."

"I do too, sir," Hexdall said. "I also would like to officially say that I am fully confident I could do this on my own."

"You two will work well together," Dermot said. "I have faith in both of you to find a way."

He made a signal. The blades of the Seahawk began turning, and in a moment the wind started messing up my hair.

Hexdall climbed in first, carrying his briefcase. I paused and said to Dermot, "Thanks for coming to get me from the island. I mean it. Thanks."

I felt suddenly awkward. A voice in my head was saying, *Hug him, hug him!* But the only time I hug someone is just before I suck out all their blood.

"You're welcome, Amber," he said. He put his arm around me, without squishing me, and drew me to his metal frame. My hand ended up on his chest, and I could feel his heart beating. He let me go. "It was a no-brainer," he continued. "I couldn't stand the thought of leaving you there."

It was, perhaps, almost a romantic thing to say. Then, a tiny pinch flustered, I stepped into the helicopter and sat across from Hexdall, and we took to the sky.

Seventeen
UP IN THE AIR

NEITHER HEXDALL NOR I SPOKE as the Seahawk made its way to Argentina, the rotors thudding like a heart in overdrive. I mostly kept my eyes closed, snoozing off and on, stirring only to look out and see that the Atlantic was still below us.

We landed at Río Gallegos, a small Argentinian port city that is on an amazingly flat stretch of land next to a river. We said goodbye to our pilot and marine escort and made our way into the airport.

"Uh, I don't have a passport," I said.

"Yes, you do." Hexdall reached into his briefcase and handed me an American passport. "Dermot had a few on file. Or he was carrying them in his suit pocket next to his heart."

What did *that* mean? I flipped the passport open. They had used the same picture as they had for other missions, though this time I was dressed in a white suit jacket they must have photoshopped. I wasn't a fan of white suit jackets—too easy to get ensanguined. I was now Angie Simmons of Albuquerque, New Mexico.

"This says I'm thirty. Thirty!"

"You've aged well." Hexdall honored me with a wide, aggravating grin. "Of course, with your kind you might be a hundred years old."

"I'm twenty-four! In real years. Not thirty."

"Well, a hundred years from now you'll be happy to be mistaken for thirty." He handed me a smartphone. "Take this. It's numbered and safe to use anywhere."

I pocketed the phone. We got through security quickly and boarded an airbus to Buenos Aires. It was packed with tourists. Maybe there was some sort of family discount, because every second seat had a child in it. It was going to be a loud flight. I'm not a huge fan of human children. They are sometimes adorable, but always far too blunt.

But my heart did nearly melt when I spotted twin girls dressed in matching blue dresses, their hair braided the same. So cute. And I couldn't help but wonder if Mom would have dressed Patty and me in similar outfits.

If we'd been raised together, that is.

Bad news: Dermot hadn't booked us seats in separate rows. Hexdall was right beside me. Good news: I successfully ignored him. Well, by *ignored* I mean I didn't talk to him, and our only interaction in the first two hours was when I stepped on his toe on the way to the washroom. It turned out he and Dermot were brothers in boredom. Hexdall spent every moment working on his smartphone with his sausage-thick fingers.

BETRAYAL

After a while I began to get aggravated that he wasn't talking to me.

"Where's my sister now?" I asked.

Hexdall looked down at me. He was certainly taller than Dermot. And probably ten years older, too, and several sizes bigger. I'm not certain why I kept comparing him to Dermot.

"We can't track her while we are in the air because there's no satellite connection. Plus, we can't turn on our Bluetooth or Wi-Fi."

"I thought that was just a silly rule the airlines made up to keep travelers docile. Be a man. Turn it on. They won't know."

"They'll know." He said this with such certainty that I didn't argue with him.

"So we won't know where she is until we land?"

"Good deduction, Sherlock."

"Well, shouldn't we be making strategies?" I asked.

"Since we don't know where she's landing or when, any plan we made would be a waste of time. When we arrive in Buenos Aires we'll get up-to-date intel, and I will make our plans from there."

"Oh," I said. I was proud that I mostly ignored his condescending tone. "Why don't you like me? Is it just because I escaped way back when you tried to capture me? Did you get demoted for that?"

"No," he said. "In fact, it was an impressive escape, since we had given you enough tranquilizer to stop an elephant. I just find you to be a loose cannon. Flighty might be another adjective that could be applied."

"I'm a freethinker. If a situation is fluid, I swim with it."

"Did you get a discount on clever sayings?" he asked. Did I mention how thick his neck is? It would take a lot to snap it. "Also, I hate vampires." He did not appear to be joking.

I was about to say a sarcastic and amazingly smart rejoinder when the plane began to shake like a paint shaker had grabbed hold of it. Turbulence. Great. I knew planes never went down because of turbulence. I'd scaled towers and rock faces and jumped out of buildings without the slightest acceleration of my heartbeat, but I couldn't stand turbulence. Several of the kids on the plane made high-pitched screaming noises. Ugh!

After an ice age, the shaking finally stopped.

"You can let go of me now," Hexdall grunted.

I looked down. My traitorous left hand had grabbed his arm. Purely a reflex. I gave him a little squeeze, digging my nails into his skin. I'll say one thing—he was tough. He didn't grimace.

"We should both rest," he said. "We'll be running at full speed soon enough."

Those were the last words he said to me on that flight. Eventually the seat-belt lights went off. And I did close my eyes, but I didn't sleep.

The plane landed, and the moment the door opened we grabbed our carry-ons—a backpack and briefcase—and followed the other passengers into the Ministro Pistarini International Airport. Rows of windows on the hangar-like building let in bright light. Giant posters hung from the ceiling, advertising perfume, lipstick and a better life.

BETRAYAL

Oh, and there were more people than you could shake a stick at. Everyone seemed to be in a hurry.

We found a bench. Hexdall opened his briefcase, shielding the screen from onlookers. He slid an earbud into his ear and said, "Uh-huh. Yes. Yes." Then he paused. "Okeydokey. "

Okeydokey? He took out the earbud.

"Was that your mom?" I asked.

"No. It was Dermot. Patty did hijack a car. She killed a woman named Mía Lopez and is using her identification now."

My sister had killed another human. I felt a chill. It was all done so casually. So easily. She was leaving a trail of bodies behind her. If every vampire was like this, no wonder Mom had left the clan.

"I'm—I'm sorry to hear that."

"She's doing what she needs to do to survive." There was perhaps begrudging respect in his tone. "We do have a lock on her location." He pointed at the screen. The blinking green dot was over the Atlantic Ocean. It showed a blue line where she had traveled and the direction it was going. Northwest. "She's on a flight to London," he said.

"You can tell, just by looking? That plane could be going anywhere in Europe. Or even Africa."

"Dermot told me. He looked up her ticket. And the tracker confirms it. It was very clever of you to use it on her."

"That's almost a compliment."

"Even a monkey can hit the right switch."

The rage was immediate, but I swallowed it. The man had no respect. He was comfortable in his larger size, forgetting that I could easily tear him apart with my vampire strength.

Well, unless he'd been augmented like Dermot.

He hit a few keys and swiped the screen. Again I was amazed that such large fingers could run a smartphone. "I have tickets for us on the next flight to London. Side by side, for your information, because it's better if someone watches over you. The flight leaves in forty minutes."

We raced through the airport to the British Airways check-in desk. As we waited in line, I got that maudlin sense that my life was about to end. I often got that just before a flight. I think it's the whole idea of putting your life in the hands of a human pilot. A human! They aren't always that trustworthy.

But sometimes you have to trust.

"You know, Hexdall, we don't have to be enemies."

He turned slightly and whispered, hiding our conversation from other ears. "I watched three of my closest friends get torn to shreds by a female vampire. She was ancient, yet so strong. And she hated us. I interviewed your father. He hates us. And just so you know, he's killed three other friends of mine. So excuse me if I'm not looking for friendship, dearie."

My father had killed some of his friends. My family was turning out to be a wrecking ball of bloodsucking death. Did he do the killings sometime before they brought him back from Iceland? Or after? It wasn't the right time to ask that question. "I'm not like my sister. I'm not like any of them, I promise you. My mom and I are different."

BETRAYAL

"The jury is out on that," he said, and it was rather gruff. "But I'll do my best to work with you because Dermot ordered me to. Just don't get in my way."

Well, that was about as close as we would come to an emotional moment. Then we were showing our electronic tickets to a tall woman in a blue suit and walking down a hallway to load ourselves onto 175,000 pounds of metal that would soon take to the air.

Thirteen hours of flying time. To show Hexdall how much I trusted him, I fell asleep beside him.

With one eye open.

Eighteen
THE TERMINAL

MY HAND ITCHED all the way down as we landed. I assumed that meant it was healing properly. I was so tempted to tear off the bandages and scratch.

It had been thirteen hours without contact from Dermot. So much could have happened in that time. Thirteen hours meant Patty could be on another plane or already on foot in another country. Dermot…well, he could have had at least three naps.

My view through the window of Heathrow Terminal 5— a monstrously and impressively tall metal and glass building—reminded me of the Crystal Palace. It seemed to me the Brits were always trying to recreate that jewel of a building. Rightfully so.

After clearing customs, we stepped into an airport pub called Huxley's and sat at a tiny two-person table. Hexdall ordered fish and chips—how unoriginal—but I guess I shouldn't criticize, since I really only had one type of meal on my personal menu.

BETRAYAL

After a lifetime of bloodsucking, I'd learned that every person has their own taste. What I wouldn't give for a good ol' oaky-flavored 1967. Or the nouveau taste of a 1998. Male or female.

I ordered myself a draft beer, my attempt at hydrating. There were now five days before I'd have to eat, and I was beginning to worry about whom I would be eating. If we spent too much time in our pursuit of Patty, I'd be hunting down a murderer on the fly. Not the easiest thing to do when you want to be sure they are guilty as charged. Oh, and unrepentant.

I was sure the Brits had their share of murderers. It was just a matter of finding the right one. Or, if I was lucky, one that tasted good. Without the fish-and-chippy smell.

Sorry, that was a stereotype.

I could eat Hexdall. That would solve a lot of problems, but I had the sneaking suspicion that Dermot would get mightily upset over that. There were already trust issues between Dermie and me—they went both ways, of course. Best if I tried to keep on the straight and narrow.

Hexdall's briefcase took up most of the table, so I had to put my glass on the edge. He was busy manhandling his tech. He punched buttons and aggressively thumbed his touch screen like he was trying to murder the phone. He did make a few grunts, which I thought were aimed at me, but I soon realized they were just his own little monologue. He slipped one of his earbuds in and began moving his lips without saying anything aloud—subvocalizing, I assumed.

At the angle I was sitting, I couldn't see what was on his screen. And it's not like I was about to slide my chair around and sit next to him. "So, what have you learned?" I asked after the third sip of my warm beer. I prefer it warm. It reminds me of blood.

"I had to reboot," he grumbled. "It's a slow process."

"Any news from Dermot?"

"Have you heard me talk to him?" he snapped, then looked maybe a pinch ashamed and said, "I can't get through. He's either in transit or away from a proper signal station. Or dead."

"I hope the likelihood of option three has a low percentage."

"Not low enough. May I remind you that someone is hunting the League? Apparently, to extinction. So excuse me if I'm testy."

His fish and chips came wrapped in waxy paper. He moved the suitcase over, bumping my beer, but with my vampiric reaction time, I caught it before it tipped over. I licked the side where it had spilled. Most men would find that erotic. Hexdall just said, "Sorry, bubs."

Bubs? To tear his head off would be such an immeasurably joyous experience.

Then he massacred the fries and fish. It was *War and Pieces*. It was like he was Ahab and was finally getting his revenge on Moby Dick. I wanted to retch—I've never much enjoyed watching humans eat. It is so unseemly. Vampires are usually neat eaters, and I take pride in rarely spilling a drop. Well, unless the prey struggles.

BETRAYAL

"There," he said, pausing to wipe a greasy finger before clicking on his smartphone. "There. There. There."

"What have you found?"

"It rebooted. And your sister's signal is alive and well and…we're in luck. She stayed in England."

I leaned closer. "Good! Where is she?"

"Oxford, it looks like. And she doesn't seem to be moving. We should get going though."

He stood up, closed the case and sniffed. "I need a washroom first," he said.

"Oh, thanks for sharing."

He ignored me and went hunting for the nearest facilities. Vampires, thankfully, are not bothered by those sorts of necessities more than once a day. One of the benefits of being a vampire.

I wandered in the general area, watching all the beating hearts of the world arrive in England. There were some fine necks. I was drawn to them, and, I must admit, saliva was beginning to pool in my mouth. Yep, definitely less than a week to go before I'd have to feed. I was hoping Dermot came through with a meal, though I wasn't certain how he'd find one so quickly. I did not want to break into a London prison. I'd done that sort of thing before, and there was so much squeezing and sneaking, and it's just not fair, like hunting animals on one of those hunting farms.

There was a terminal flashing a few feet away, and I was drawn to the large letters that said *City of London Library Services*. I went over and looked at what was essentially a large screen in the shape of a giant iPad. One thing I can't resist is books. And I, of course, know the long history of England and the English language (they invented it, after all). But I also am aware of the history of many British public and private libraries. There are librarians I knew in Seattle who booked holidays across the pond and visited library after library in England. Biblionerds to the core.

And I would have traveled with them in a heartbeat.

So I learned from the terminal that the city of London has the Barbican Children's Library, the Guildhall Library (a reference library specializing in the history of London) and several others. They even have home delivery! The idea of it. Sitting at home, a pot of steaming tea and Jeeves dropping by to hand over my next read and take the old read home. Heaven!

I clicked on a few more links, poking around the information sections. I had been keeping up with my classes online (and using a byway on the dark internet so I couldn't be tracked), but this last week or so of traveling had put me behind. I was writing an essay with the title "Underprivileged Paper," all about the effects of digital filing on the purchase and collecting of actual, real books in libraries.

I missed it. The calmness of thinking library thoughts. The joy of chasing knowledge and not just blood.

The screen flashed. It was almost a subliminal flash, just below perception. Then a pop-up popped up.

You're our 1066th visitor. Congratulations! If your name is William, we'll be doubly impressed.

BETRAYAL

Yep, that was the date of William the Conqueror invading England. They are clever coders, these London librarians.

Please take this quick quiz.

I clicked the Yes button.

You are obviously a wise book lover. A wise reader. What is your favorite book?

I typed in *Charlotte's Web*. It has stuck with me since the day Mom read it to me when I was eight. I still remember the thrill of that story. Mom had likely read other books aloud to me, but that is the first I truly remember. I can still picture the wallpaper. The room. It was likely the twentieth house we'd lived in, since we were always fleeing.

Thanks for reading it to me, Mom!

The screen flashed with: **Wise choice. A true classic. So much can be said about a reader from their choice in books. Though we try not to judge a reader by their cover. Who is your favorite author?**

There was no hesitation. ***Shirley Jackson.***

The Haunting of Hill House. "The Lottery." Prose infused with the ghostly presence of fear.

Well, that summed Jackson up.

Please look closely at the screen. Lean in.

I did so. Not certain where this little quiz was taking me.

There was the faintest red flash. Then a ghostly figure popped up and flew straight toward me, and I swear, it went right past my shoulder and out. I looked to the left and shuddered. There wasn't a sign of it.

Gotcha! That was one of Jackson's haunters.

I leaned back. It was clever, and they really had gotten me. But there was something about that red light that reminded me of something else. I couldn't quite place my finger on it.

Shirley Jackson is available at the following libraries. Please do pay us a visit.

It listed several libraries, including the Barbican and the other nicely named Shoe Lane Library.

Thank you for—

The screen went blank, the machine buzzed, and a shock zapped into my fingertips. The screen flashed again with these words.

Are you in trouble? Do you need our help?

Well, that was an odd little algorithm glitch. Perhaps the coders weren't as clever as I'd thought.

We know who you are. You are not safe. We will come to you. You must complete your studies.

What the hell? It did seem to be specific to me. Well, they hadn't said my name, but the mention of studies was almost specific.

I tried to type something.

System Error. System Error.

It rebooted and came back with the same screen. It said, **Welcome, visitor number 1067.** But no matter how much I clicked, all I found were pages about the City Business Library.

"You playing a game?"

I nearly spun around and took off Hexdall's head.

"Whoa! Touchy. Must be that time of month…and by that, I mean feeding time. Are you ready to go?"

BETRAYAL

"Yes." I gave the iPad terminal thingy another glance. Perhaps it was nothing more than a coder's joke, but the hairs on the back of my neck were raised.

We know who you are. You are not safe.

I followed Hexdall out of Terminal 5 and into a cab.

Nineteen

LOOK BEFORE YOU LEAP

THE CAB WAS ONE of the stereotypical small black cabs you see in British movies. They look cute on the screen but are cramped in real life, and this one smelled like an old sock. I still found it odd that the driver was on the opposite side, but that seemed to be working out for the Brits.

Hexdall waved a stack of fifty-pound notes in front of the driver. "Will that get us to Oxford? Quickly?"

The driver nodded solemnly, not even raising his eyebrows. British nonchalance apparently ran in his blood. The trip would take at least an hour, so I assumed he was making a tidy profit.

We left the airport, pulling onto the M25—a highway with several lanes of traffic. Again, all on the wrong side. I couldn't help but think I'd walked into an alternate world where everything was a reflection of the real world. London was to my right, and I felt some regret we weren't heading straight into that city. I'd cut my literary teeth reading books that featured

BETRAYAL

good ol' London town. Dickens had walked those streets. And James Bond. Well, not Bond so much as Ian Fleming. And this was the land of J.K. Rowling and J.R.R. Tolkien too.

So I have a soft spot in my heart for England. Mom never wanted to move here, because she thought we'd stand out with our accents. It would be harder for us to blend in if every time we opened our mouths, the polite, stone-faced Brits thought, Ugh, Americans. Go back to the colonies.

"Yes. Yes," Hexdall said. At first I thought he was talking to himself, but then I saw he had slipped his earbud in. "An order? Then yes, here she is."

He passed the earbud to me. I looked at it, wondering how much wax it might have on it. I wiped it on my pants and pressed it into my ear. "Hello?"

"Hello, Amber," a ragged, frail voice replied. It sounded like an old lady.

"Who is this?"

"It's me, Dermot," the voice said. Once he'd said his name, I could hear that it really was him.

"You sound like hell."

"My recovery is not going as planned. We've run several tests. It seems the paralytic agent your sister injects has a few other serious side effects that yours doesn't. I'm losing muscle mass rather quickly." He inhaled, a rattling, raspy breath. "It's like catching a wasting disease."

"Well, eat up. Or drink protein power shakes." Even as I said it, I realized I was sounding rather flippant. "Really, take care of yourself, Dermot."

"I—I will. I wanted to let you know that I've gone through the League papers that I can access. I can't find any clearly moral hunts for you in England. There's one in Zimbabwe, but that's not helpful. I know this must be frustrating."

"It is. I had my next meal in Mexico all planned out." I licked my lips and couldn't help but glance at Hexdall's neck.

"I'm sorry about that." Dermot coughed. "I know we still have a few days, and of course you have to find Patty, but do you have other options?"

"A prison is my usual standby. I don't suppose we have an extra few days so I could do the proper research to find a good, moral meal."

"There isn't time. We need to find your sister while we still have the ability to track her. She could disappear at any moment."

"Yes, I know that." My left hand had tightened on my leg, nails poking into my skin. I was hungry! "I do appreciate you, um, shopping for meals for me."

"It's not something I ever imagined doing. But I guess one learns to adapt to the current situation."

"It's like you're trying to take me out for dinner."

That got a weak laugh out of him. "Yes, something like that."

"Well, keep trying. What are your plans for Patty? Once we catch up with her."

"Well, we have to assume she doesn't know we're following her and that we have surprise on our side. I have no intel on why she would go to Oxford. Perhaps there is a safe

BETRAYAL

house there or she has friends or family—which, of course, makes the situation even more dangerous. I am scrabbling together a capture team."

"Not sure I like that word *scrabbling*."

"Funds and resources are low, Amber. But I'll be able to get some good men and women together. Your goal should be to observe and not engage until the team arrives."

"I'm sure we'll do our best to do that," I said.

"Michael knows that. Trust him. I know you two don't get along but—"

"That's an understatement."

"Trust him. I do. Oh, and don't do anything stupid."

I narrowed my eyes, hoping he could feel my glare from across the ocean. "What does that mean?"

"I mean look before you leap. That's all."

"Jeez, you sound like my mom. I know I can be rather hasty sometimes."

"We all need to enter this mission clearheaded. Each decision must be logical."

He was implying that I was not logical. I would have argued with him if I hadn't left my shoe at the hit in Burj Khalifa. That simple mistake had led to the death of a shoe-store employee and an attack on my apartment. I still shuddered when I thought of poor Genevieve. Oh, and I had compromised the other hit in Iceland just slightly—hmm, maybe he was right to be worried. Well, I'd made up for those mistakes. And I did have months more of training, including the wushu I'd taken in Mexico. That ancient Chinese martial art had included endless hours of qigong breathing and relaxation techniques. They were helpful.

"I'll do my best to be logical," I said. "It's not my forte, apparently."

"I'm not intending to offend you, Amber." He coughed a phlegmy, death-rattle cough right after this statement.

"Take care of yourself, Dermot. Please."

"I will," he said. "You do the same. Over and out."

I handed the earbud back to Hexdall. He made a show of wiping it on his pants, then inserted it back into his ear. "Yes. Yes, sir." A long pause. "Yep, I'll keep an eye on her."

I was being babysat. I huffed, felt a blast of angst and anger and then did a bit of qigong breathing and looked out the window. The green pastures of England gradually calmed me.

I was centered by the time we got to Oxford. My *sifu* would have been proud.

Twenty
CORONATION STREET, WITH FANGS

THE CITY OF OXFORD looks intelligent. It has all the typical old Victorian buildings, the vines and various greenery that one associates with jolly ol' England, but there is also a sense that the people are smarter. That the conversations they are having in tea shops or on the street don't have any *ums* or *uhs* in them, but a sprinkling of *forthright* and *rather*.

Oxford University is home to the Bodleian Libraries. That sounds like a word Tolkien would have made up, but if you were a librarian, your inner librarian nerd would begin to salivate upon hearing that name. When you can boast that your main library, the Bod, has been around for over four hundred years, well, them's cool bragging rights.

"Take a left at the next intersection," Hexdall said to the cabbie. He was looking at his fancy smartphone, as usual. After we zipped down that street and followed a few more of his instructions, Hexdall said, "This is where we get out."

And we did, each holding our travel bags. Hexdall handed the money to the cab driver, and the car drove away.

"It looks like *Coronation Street*," I said.

"What street?" Hexdall asked.

"Oh, it was a show I watched a few times when I was in Canada. It seemed to be on every channel. Very soap opera-ish. I'm sure it's not up your alley...or your street."

He grimaced. "I'm sure it isn't. We'll be staying here." He pointed. It was a brick building with blue shutters on each window and a little white sign that said *River Hotel*. They had taken the word *quaint* and built it with brick.

We went to check in, and I saw another one of those library terminals in the corner. I put my hand on it, and it came to life. **Would you like books delivered to your room?** I pulled my hand away. They actually delivered books to hotels? I wasn't certain about that. I backed away from it.

One credit card swipe later, we were in our rooms. Mine had a single bed with a green quilt. Not the largest room, but comfy.

My hand had begun to itch to the point that I couldn't ignore it anymore. I went into the bathroom and removed the bandages to discover that the spear wound had mostly healed. It wasn't quite time to take out the stitches. The hand was weaker and felt slower, but I was sure once the nerves had regenerated, it would be fine. I yawned.

I stretched out on the bed. Forty winks would do me well and take my mind off the hunger that was starting to build in my stomach. I closed my eyes.

BETRAYAL

A moment later someone gave my door a sharp knock. I leaped up, confused about how the room had gotten so dark in such a short period of time. As I reached to unlock the door, I could hear the familiar meaty heartbeat of Hexdall. He did have a rather large heart, that was clear. I opened the door.

"You keep things dark," Hexdall commented.

The sun had set. My nap had apparently turned into an hours-long sleep. I blinked and did that act you do when you want to pretend you didn't just wake up. "I have good night vision, and it's good. Really, it is." I sounded more drunk than tired.

Hexdall lifted one of his caterpillar eyebrows. "Yes, I suppose you do." *Nappus interruptus*, I'd call him. He opened his briefcase on the dresser, and it took a moment for the screen to come on. "The target is not far from here," he said. "And the signal has stopped moving. She has been settled down in a small warehouse for the last eight hours."

"Good. Maybe she's asleep. What's your plan?" I didn't say *our* plan on purpose.

"Our plan," he said, as if he were reading my mind, "is to take a look-see." The word sounded funny when he said it, like his mouth wasn't meant to use cutesy words. "We just have to scout before the wet team comes."

"You meant capture team, right? Doesn't wet team imply there will be a death?"

"Yes, a capture team. But there may be wet work, if things go south. Or if she has allies. Let's hope it doesn't come to that. You'll be the eyes and ears, and I'll be the brain."

"I'll be all three, thanks," I said. I was obviously still sleepy.

"We can only work together if you listen to me." He said this slowly. Then he handed me my very own earbud. Next, he handed me a black dot. "This earbud has a range of three miles, plenty of distance. We'll be able to communicate. Put the dot next to your Adam's apple—well, that general area—and it will pick up any words you subvocalize. The earbud—"

"Goes in my ear. I get it."

"You're a smart girl." I'm not sure calling me *girl* was an improvement on *bubs*. "Put it in."

I did so. It fit perfectly. Hexdall's throat and mouth moved, and I heard in one ear, "Are you receiving?"

"Yes," I said aloud.

"Subvocalize. It's basically talking without making noise."

"I know what it is," I said, and then I subvocalized this clever line: "Hexdall is a poisonous bunch-backed toad."

"Well, at least you use Shakespearian insults." He did not sound entertained.

"Color me impressed! You know your bard."

"You're looking at an English major." I was nearly flabbergasted. "*Richard III* is where that comes from," he continued. "After my arts degree, I got into engineering, but before I could finish my studies, a little ol' invite from the FBI came my way. The rest is history. Well, history that's been blacked out." He paused as if he were expecting a laugh. "You will experience some lack of hearing in the ear with the earbud. I also, hesitantly, give you this."

He handed me a smartwatch. There was no branding on it. It showed the time: 8:45 PM. "What's it do?"

"It tells time. Also, tap the button on the side three times."

I did so, and the screen showed the map of a building. It took me a moment to realize it was a map of the hotel, all in glowing green. There was a red dot at the front desk. And two red dots in my room. "It's a scanner!"

"Yes, something like that. It sends out a low-frequency radar pulse every few seconds. And it can track some movement. It allows you to see through walls as long as there's something moving on the other side."

"Wow, this is amazingly high-tech for the League."

"I designed it," he said. Not without some pride. "It also is tuned to the tracker on Patty. When you get closer, it will glow green and show her exact location."

"Good work, Hexdall. I'm completely impressed."

"Yes, well, that's nice." He looked like he was trying to summon up something gruff to say, but failed. "Let's go over the plan."

Then he told it to me.

Fifteen minutes later, dressed in black, I left the hotel alone and walked down the cobblestone sidewalk. I opened and closed my right hand to keep it limber. "Test one," he said in my ear.

"Test received," I subvocalized.

"Good. Now let's go silent."

Well, I could do that. The plan was rather simple, though it took him several minutes to explain every detail that he

ARTHUR SLADE

had ascertained about the building. But basically I was just supposed to poke around and observe.

When I was two blocks from the address he'd given me, I climbed a bare brick wall to the top of an old apartment building. I made my way to a position where I could look down on the warehouse. It was next to an office supply store. Of course, even the storage depots looked fancy in this city. The small warehouse was all bricks and vines. I wouldn't have been surprised to see Bilbo and his hobbit clan walk out the front door. A big sign on the largest door said simply *SHIPPING*.

None of the main-level lights were on. What could be offices or apartments on the second floor were also dark, except one glowing light that illuminated a white blind. It seemed to have holes in it. They may have been bullet holes.

Or it was moth-eaten.

I had leaned up against a chimney, hiding in the shade. Pale skin did tend to catch the moonlight and reflect other city lights.

"I'm in position," I said.

"Give me a description of what you see."

I did so, feeling like a real-estate agent. "There aren't any hobbits," I added at the end. He didn't laugh.

"Can you tell what floor she's on with your little doohickey?" I asked. I remembered to subvocalize. I also got a kick out of saying the word *doohickey*.

"No."

Hexdall wasn't really gifted at extrapolating. I looked at my watch, but the building was too far away for me to scan it. "Well, what do we do now?"

BETRAYAL

"Just observe. It's so simple even you can do it."

And so I did. I watched without moving, trying not to even blink. The building sat stark still, like a building does. The occasional drunk or young partier wandered by, looking for a pub or a place to pee. A car puttered down the street. Other than that, it was a still image.

"Nothing is happening," I said after twenty minutes.

"Patience is a virtue," Hexdall replied. He was particularly gifted at pressing my buttons.

I stared. And stared and stared.

Then, to my surprise, the front door opened, and Patty walked out. She stood about three feet from the door and glanced around the street. Then she stared up in my direction. I held completely still, willing even my heart to stop.

"Patty is at the front door," I subvocalized. "She's looking directly at me."

"Don't move."

"I'm not."

Patty lifted an arm and pointed at me. I felt like she was using a laser pointer. Then she gestured at the street in what I assumed was a *Get down here, sis* gesture. Finally she curled her finger, inviting me inside.

"She just signaled me inside."

"Ignore her. We've been compromised. We are going to have to wait for the extraction team and hope she sticks around."

"I can't wait. We could lose her."

Hexdall spoke more gruffly than Billy Goat Gruff from the fairy tale. "I'm going to say this slowly, Amber, so you understand. Come back to the hotel *now*. Do not go inside that building. That is an order."

Guess he didn't say it slow enough. Or he forgot I'm not so great at taking orders.

Twenty-One
FOUR REASONS WHY I SHOULD HAVE LISTENED TO HEXDALL

I DIDN'T FOLLOW MY SISTER'S suggestion either. No way was I going in the front door. Instead I ran almost a block down the rooftop, jumped across to the row of buildings that held the warehouse, and climbed down the opposite side to a darkened window. My hand still wasn't quite opening and closing correctly, but I managed to do it all without falling or making a sound.

Well, there was one constant sound. The whole time, Hexdall was spouting off in my ear. There was a lot of "Stand down," "Get back here right now," "I'm going to strangle you" and other joyful blurtings. I tuned them out, wishing for volume control. I didn't want to toss the earpiece away. He was my lifeline, after all. And, I must admit, I kind of got a kick out of his anger.

There was likely some sort of alarm system on the window, so I used my ol' *cut through glass with my fingernail* trick, making a large enough square for me to step through.

I drilled one small hole and held the glass in place while I cut the square and pulled the perfectly sliced glass out and set it gently on the windowsill. The last thing I needed was to drop it and have it smash on the street. Then I slowly pushed aside the curtain.

Inside was a darkened office. A computer left over from the late '90s sat on a desk littered with papers. The monitor was one of those massive CRT displays—probably even too advanced for the League. There were scads of crumpled papers on the floor. I sniffed, catching a good whiff of the smell of too much human sweat. It seemed to be leaking out of the walls. I listened for heartbeats. Nothing. Then I stepped in. The floor creaked despite my slight weight. There was nothing I could do about that.

I'll admit I was acting stupid. But nobody bit Dermot and got away with it! My other reasons were twofold. I couldn't wait. And I wanted to see Patty on my own for a moment. To give her a chance. Yes, I know she stabbed me. But she could have aimed for my heart, so I was thankful she hadn't killed me. And if we waited, she'd be long gone. I'd be sure to always stay near an exit. I was proud but not crazy. I was pretty certain I could outrun her—well, let's say 87 percent certain.

And she'd signaled to me. A sister deserved one more chance. Then I'd knock her out and truss her up and deliver her to Hexdall, as long as there was a promise she wouldn't be hurt, and I'd have full access to her. No wet work!

I pressed the button on my high-tech watch, and it displayed the walls around me. No one was moving in

BETRAYAL

the hallway, so I opened the office door and glanced back and forth. I didn't want to totally trust the tech. There were two more doors on the opposite side of the hallway, the offices I'd viewed from across the street. I peeked through the keyhole into the one that was lit. Yes, it was a door so old that it had a keyhole.

It provided a surprisingly clear view of an empty room. Someone had just left the lights on. And another glance at my watch confirmed the top floor was empty. Not even a mouse stirring, which meant Patty was waiting downstairs in the warehouse proper. Her tracker hadn't appeared on-screen yet, which made me wonder how close I'd have to get to her before that happened.

At the end of the hallway was a stairway that led to the warehouse floor. I did my favorite trick. I crawled down the ceiling of the stairwell, digging my nails into the slats. Again, not so easy with my sore hand, and I wondered at my wisdom here. After all, except for that minor injury to her posterior, my sister was healthy. And she'd at least had some blood recently. I was getting hungry.

Too late to back out now, and at least Hexdall had stopped his shouting. My mental map of the warehouse reminded me that there were four windows. If things got too hot, it would be easy enough to jump through one of them, roll onto the street, dodge a few lorries and be gone. I might even stop to bring fish and chips in newspaper as a peace offering to Hexdall.

No one met me at the bottom of the stairwell. It opened into a warehouse stacked with bundles of paper, bins of pencils and the usual paraphernalia you'd find in any stationery store. The lack of heartbeats was frustrating. If Patty was here, and I didn't know why she wouldn't be, she was masking her heartbeat. I climbed down the side of the wall and sneaked behind a wooden crate. My eyes were perfectly adjusted to the dark. I made my way around another crate. And another. And past a box of packing tape.

Why the hell would she invite me in here and not stick around to chat?

I noted that the windows behind me were blocked by crates. That meant there were now only two windows I could jump through. Or, if necessary, I could flee through the front door.

I looked at my little smartwatch, using one hand to block the light it cast. It blipped, showing a green dot that proved she was in the room with me. In fact, good ol' Patty was only a few steps away. She should have been right in front of me.

But she wasn't. Unless she was invisible.

A tiny flashing attracted my attention. I looked down and leaned over. A toy crab-like thing was on the floor and flashing.

The tracker.

She'd taken it out and set it here. Patty wanted me to stand in this exact spot. Shit!

Next came four sounds. *Thup. Thup. Thup. Thup.*

Two on either side of me. One in front, one behind.

It was four enemies landing, silent as cats. They had dropped from the ceiling and surrounded me. I looked up, ever so slowly.

BETRAYAL

A man was looking down at me. He was white, tall, in his thirties and dressed in what might have been a tactical-operations dry suit—a uniform SWAT teams wear. His smile was impressively wide.

So wide it showed his fangs.

Twenty-Two
HORNSWOGGLED AND HOG-TIED

A QUICK GLANCE to either side showed a male and a female vampire with similar smiles and dressed in similar dark suits. I could hear their heartbeats now, but something about the suits had muffled them from a distance. I could only assume the one behind me was also smiling.

"Um," I subvocalized, "hey, darling Hexdall...I may be in trouble. Four vampires. Surrounded."

"Hello," I said aloud.

"Greetings, sister," the man in front of me said. I was really hoping he was using *sister* congenially and not literally. I'd met enough of my family already.

"Uh, hello, bro," I answered. "I have this sneaking suspicion you were expecting me."

"Let's just say we were certain you'd drop by."

I noticed he was holding what looked to be a pole with a large manacle on the end. Its purpose wasn't clear to me, but I also didn't want to know. The other two were holding their own manacles on poles. The fourth was most likely also armed that way.

Patty strode out from behind a bin filled with boxes of paper clips. "Ah, Amber, you came alone. That was wise. No interfering humans. This can be a sister-to-sister visit."

I pointed at the tracker on the floor. "When did you discover the tracker?"

"About an hour into my flight to Buenos Aires. Let's just say I wasn't comfortable in my seat. One quick bathroom inspection later, I had that electronic crab out of me and in my pocket. Then a brilliant plan popped into my head that has now come to fruition."

"You wanted to lead me all the way here? To meet your four friends. All five of you vampires, I should say." I was aware that Hexdall was hearing at least my half of the conversation. I hoped he could put it together.

"Yes. That was part of my plan. Though I was hoping the last of your League would travel with you. Kill two birds with one stone, so to speak."

"Was it vampires who destroyed the League's HQ?"

"No," Patty said. "We tend to leave drained bodies and aren't so big on armaments or guns, for that matter. But we were happy to hear about it through the grapevine."

"Keep them talking," Hexdall said in my ear. "I'm coming."

"No. It's too much of a risk," I subvocalized.

"Duck when I tell you to," Hexdall said. "Just listen to me this once."

"Stay back," I subvocalized.

ARTHUR SLADE

"Do you have some sort of problem?" Patty said. "You keep moving your mouth."

"Temporomandibular joint disorder," I said, rubbing my jaw. I credited my library studies for allowing me to come up with big words like that on the spot. Plus, one of my fellow students in Seattle had the jaw-joint disorder. "I'm a tooth grinder. And I bite through any retainers." I did show her my fangs.

She looked at me like I was perhaps a little insane. "Well, whatever, sis. I—"

Then she leaped. And before I could react, she poked at my neck and jumped back. She looked at the black dot she'd scraped from my skin. "A subvocalizer. Well, goody, you're not alone. I'd say he's talking in your ear right now."

"What's happening?" Hexdall said.

I wanted to shush him, but there wasn't any point. He wouldn't hear me.

"I was broadcasting live on YouTube," I said.

"You know, you're only half as clever as you think you are," my sister said. "I believe that comes from spending a lot of time alone. Jokes are funny to an audience of one. Or maybe Mom told you that you were funny. She lied."

So this is what it was like to have a big sister? "Let's cut to the chase then," I said. "What is it you want from me? To come back to vampire land and join you and these hissing sissies? Then we'll all live happily ever after in a big castle, passing our time hunting down humans?"

The male vampire in front of me did hiss in a good-natured fashion. And Patty outright laughed. I wondered

BETRAYAL

if my laugh sounded like hers, because it was grating and high-pitched, and I was regretting my decision to give her a chance. Actually, I was regretting not listening to Hexdall.

"You have an over-inflated sense of your importance, sister," Patty said. "There's only one thing we want from you, and it's inside you."

"Excuse me?"

"You are not the smartest branch of the Fang tree." She put her hands on her hips. "You don't know why we've been pursuing Mom all these years. Does one vampire with a lame-brained moral code really matter? Yet we have been hunting her day and night for over twenty years—almost your whole lifetime. Don't you wonder why ZARC Industries has spent billions to develop systems to capture vampires? You have no idea at all, do you?"

"Of course, I do," I said. The words were weak. "It's—" Ah, I couldn't come up with anything. I had no idea why they were chasing us, other than some odd hope of using our genetic material.

I glanced up at the ceiling, wondering if I could leap out over them. Me against five vampires. To misquote Katniss, the odds were never in my favor.

"You seem to be looking to escape," Patty said. She snapped her fingers, and the vampire man in front of me pushed out with the manacle thing, and I blocked his blow. But it was a feint, because the two on either side of me manacled my arms, and the one behind grabbed me by the neck. The guy in front clamped his locking device around my leg. I tried to push up, to pull, but they had me from every direction. I gave it my all, swearing, sweating, spitting and jerking left and right as hard as I could. I was hog-tied and hornswoggled.

Then the electric shocks began. My captors were strong enough to hold me upright as I jerked and spasmed and smashed my teeth together. My hair was likely standing straight up. But I could see, through it all, that my sister was grinning.

When the shocks came to an end, she added a verbal one. "We want your ovaries, sis."

Twenty-Three
THE LILITH AFFAIR

"HUH?" WAS ALL I COULD MANAGE. In my defense, I'd just had the whole UK power grid sent through my body. My eyes were watering, my jaws were trembling, and my muscles were jittering. I stopped struggling.

I didn't slump though. They held me tightly, but I managed to also hold myself up.

"What the hell are you talking about?" I said once I could put a cogent thought together.

"The hell I'm talking about is a little bit of invasive surgery. Heck, what's a little bit of spilled blood when you're talking about the future of vampirekind? You've been away from the family for some time, Amber—the black sheep with a heart of gold. And you won't know this about vampires. We are having a teensy-weensy fertility problem."

"Go to a clinic," I said. "Grab an egg."

Her grin looked so much like mine it was uncanny. "Oh, believe me, we've tried. We've tried. Every medical

ARTHUR SLADE

avenue has been pursued by the Grand Council. And we have some of the best doctors in the world in our fold. When you can study for two hundred years, you can learn a lot. But the relative truth, my sweet relative, is that there has been a precipitous drop in new vampires being born. I won't bore you with sperm counts, because I don't know if Mommy taught you the birds and the bees. But I will give you one important fact: you're the last vampire to have been born."

"I am?" My words echoed.

"Yes!" She hissed the word. "I suppose Mom told you that you were special. Well, she was telling the truth. So very true. And having a near-zero birth rate is not horrible for vampires. We do live for hundreds of years, but we're only fertile for the first hundred or so. That's another fact you may not know. Eventually that little statistic will come back to bite us in the behind. There will be no more vampires."

So that's why Mom had fled. Hiding from other vampires. Perhaps she thought she could start a new, moral strain and in time the old strain would die out. "So you want my *eggs*?"

"Yes," she said rather nonchalantly. I expected her to rub her hands together in glee. "But more than that, we want your whole reproductive system. All of it. That's why we were looking for Mom. She was the last to give birth and still has a good thirty years of fertility in her. If you have the same anti-resistant eggs, you'll be as valuable as her. Your body parts will be, that is. The rest of you, not so much."

"So I take it your eggs are duds?"

BETRAYAL

An *I just drank sour milk* look flashed across her face. "Like I said, you're special, Amber. Very special. And we're going to take the special parts out of you and put them in a fertility container we call Lilith."

"Lilith? Adam's first wife." I'd always liked the name and her story.

"Yes, we're being clever. There are some who say Lilith was the mother of all vampires. Now it will become truth. In a way, you'll be Lilith. Although, sadly, you won't survive the removal. It's a very invasive technique. But don't worry, this Lilith machine we've cooked up is fully capable of recreating your ovulation, and other vampires will carry the children to term. Your children, that is. Oh, and raise them with the proper moral codes."

I pictured an army of Ambers spreading destruction around the world. This was all getting a little too personal. I've only thought about having children a few times. Mostly I am too busy running for my life. Plus, as far as I know, I need a male vampire to make the whole baby-making part work. But I wasn't about to let other female vampires have my eggs. They weren't going to have any part of me.

"You can't do this. I forbid it."

Her cackle was truly evil and not all that sisterly. "Yes, we can. And we will. You really should look at this as saving your own kind. You'll produce enough eggs to keep us going for years. And if we can crack your fertility system, we will have solved the fertility problem. Maybe we'll be able to take our true place at the world table. The dominant place with blood bags as our servants. We'll put a plaque up about you, don't worry."

"It's wrong, it's just—"

"Duck," a voice barked in my ear. "Amber, duck now."

"What?" I said. Then I remembered. "Oh, yeah."

I pulled myself down to the ground, quite suddenly and with all the strength I could summon out of my weary muscles. It was enough to surprise my captors. Though they'd been holding me tightly, I was able to get at least halfway down to my haunches.

"What are you—" Patty began.

The first bullet caught the grinning vampire in front of me in the head. The second bullet caught the vampire beside me. She thudded to the floor. The third bullet missed.

Not because Dermot was a bad shot. But because vampire number three had flattened and skittered across the floor like a centipede on speed. The vampire behind me dropped the clamp for my neck but was winged in the shoulder before she leaped behind a crate.

Patty had an angry look on her face. "Do I have to kill everyone myself?" she said. Then she was flipping, spinning away as shots hit the floor a moment after she'd left. She was faster than me. It hurt to admit it.

Dead male vampire and dead female vampire apparently had some sort of clutch reflex, because they hadn't dropped their clamps. I had to yank hard to get them out of their hands before using brute vampiric force to snap the metal clamps and free myself and my ovaries from their clutches.

BETRAYAL

Hexdall was kneeling at the front door, dressed all in black and swinging his scoped rifle back and forth. He signaled me to come to him. "Run, Amber. This way."

I tossed away the last of the manacles and glanced around. All three remaining vampires had vanished, including Patty. I clacked speedily toward Hexdall.

Clacked because I'd missed one of the clamps on my leg, and it was smashing into the concrete floor as I ran. It must have looked like a sped-up silent comedy film. Charlie Chaplin would have been impressed. I skidded to a stop, reached down and unclamped it.

Then I looked up and pointed as quickly as I could, trying to warn Hexdall. Patty had crept across the ceiling and was directly above him. He was still crouched and motioning to me, looking left and right.

She came down on him like two tons of fury.

Twenty-Four

IS THIS YOUR NUMBER?

SHE DID NOT LAND SOFTLY.

One of her feet caught the gun, and it fell to the the floor. Her other foot smashed his head, and Hexdall crumbled down, managing only a partial blocking motion. Before he could get back up, she had her claws out, tearing like mad at his uniform. His flesh.

I ran full speed toward him.

But Hexdall hadn't trained for nothing. He caught Patty with an uppercut that threw her off him. She landed on her feet and was right back at him, whirling, punching, biting. She clamped her teeth to his arm, searching for the brachial artery, but it's not easy to get. Even missing the artery, the bite would still inject a bit of her paralytic agent, and that would slow him.

Hexdall didn't show any immediate effects. He ripped her off his arm and jujitsued her into the wall behind him. Then he drew a mean-looking blade from his belt.

BETRAYAL

By that point, I was leaping to join the fray.

Alas, my leap was interrupted by a hand that grabbed my left foot, and I thudded hard onto the cement floor. I twisted to see that a female vampire had hold of me. She was built more like a football player and had linebacker strength. She yanked me toward her.

I shot up onto one leg, found my balance and said hello with my fist, smacking her jaw. Only at that moment did I remember my hand was still healing. And though her head snapped back with a satisfied crack, my hand reverberated with pain, and blood seeped out from where I'd been wounded. I shook my hand, took a moment to clear my head and, as the vampire closed in on me again, I thought about my legs.

More directly, I thought about using them. I performed a front-leg axe kick that caught her jaw, and she staggered back. Obviously, this vampire had relied on stealth and strength. I faked my following kick and then caught her with a round-house that knocked her out.

By this time Patty had been joined by the last remaining vampire—a male—and between the two of them, they'd disarmed Hexdall, caught both of his hands and were doing their best to pull him apart. My angle brought me into the male vampire, who deftly guided me past him and into the side of a crate. But he'd let go of Hexdall to do it.

I got up and dispatched the vampire handily. Well, footily. And was rather impressed with myself for a moment, but when I turned, I saw that Patty had Hexdall in a headlock. "One more step, and I'll snap his neck," she said.

I stayed still.

"Don't listen to her," Hexdall barked. "My neck's too thick to snap." His face was a mass of bruises, but he managed a grin. "Besides, I'd suggest slowly backing away. I've engaged a fragmentation device. Dermot would never forgive me if you were fragmented."

He was talking about a grenade. By the look on his face I knew he was serious. I backed away.

"Don't move," Patty said. "He's bluffing."

But there was something blinking in his pocket. I couldn't quite tell what it was. "He doesn't bluff. Believe me. He's not smart enough to bluff."

He grabbed on tight to Patty's hand. She tried to pull it away, but he cemented his grip. I was pretty certain his strength was augmented—otherwise, there'd have been no way he could hold Patty still.

"I'm sorry I called you an ass," I said as I continued walking backward.

He grinned. "I deserved it."

I kept backing up. I really was hoping he was bluffing. He hugged the struggling Patty like they were long-lost lovers.

The thing went off.

There was no explosion. Instead a green gas burst out of his pocket, surrounding them both. She coughed, he coughed, and soon they vanished in the thick fog that was spreading through the storage area.

The male vampire I'd just dealt with stood up, saw the gas and tried to move, but the moment it touched him,

BETRAYAL

he collapsed. Now that was potent stuff! I had no idea what was in the gas, so I ran toward the other side of the room. When I was there, I quickly glanced back.

The gas had already mostly dissipated. Hexdall was on the floor. Patty was wandering away from him, rubbing at her eyes and running into walls. She was clearly tougher than I'd given her credit for. Tougher than me.

Hexdall was clearly dead. His neck was twisted too far to one side.

Patty tripped over the other vampire and smacked into a column.

The smell of the gas was making my eyes water, and even in this weakened state, I couldn't assume it wasn't poisonous. Doziness was threatening to take over my thoughts.

I stumbled through the crates to the back door. I didn't know if Hexdall had intended to sacrifice himself. At the very least, he'd come to rescue me. He had been a dependable man, despite his antipathy toward me. And I'd let him down! Why had I tried to take Patty on by myself?

There was nothing I could do about that now, and no sense in making his sacrifice for nothing. I reached for the back door.

But before I could twist the handle, I was slammed to the floor. "You're not going anywhere."

At first I thought it was Patty. But the distance between her and me was too great. It was the muscular lady vampire with a massive grump on. She grabbed my arm and twisted it behind me and ground my face into the cement, doing her very best

147

to use the floor as a cheese grater. My face being the cheese. I tried to untwist my limb and break the hold but failed.

Then two feet stumbled into my line of vision. I glanced up with one eye, because the other was quite close to the cement. Patty was standing above me, her face green. Either the gas had stained her, or the green was from lack of breath. She stamped her foot down on my face and held my head in place.

"Now where were we, sis?" she said. "Oh yes, I believe we were discussing the removal of your innards."

The word *innards* rang around and around my head. It sounded so old-fashioned. And horrible. I reached for something snappy to say, but the only snappy thing was my arm being twisted near to breaking. All the kung fu in the world isn't helpful if you are trapped.

Patty kicked me in the ribs, knocking the breath out of my lungs. Then she kicked me again. And again. And again. I couldn't move out of the way. Nor could I catch even the slightest bit of air.

"Aarrgh," I said. In a moment I wouldn't have a single rib left.

"I can't believe Mom chose you over me," she hissed. "That even biology chose you over me. It's so fucking unfair."

Her boots were obviously steel-toed. Big Bertha was holding me in place. I felt a darkness—the pain was so deep that it was washing over all my other senses. Maybe it would be best if I blacked out.

Which is when I started hearing voices.

BETRAYAL

"Is your library card number 121435?" a female said in my ear. At first I thought Patty was insane and spouting something about my library card. Then I realized the voice I'd heard was in my earbud.

"Whus?" I said. It was actually more of a moan. I turned my head enough to see that Hexdall hadn't moved from where he was lying. Still dead. Which didn't explain how someone had spoken in my earbud.

"What was that about my library card?" I chugged each word out and somehow completed the sentence.

"What the hell are you talking about?" Patty asked. "Oh, never mind." Then she stomped on my spine. Apparently, my back wasn't needed for their little fertility experiment.

"Is your library card number 121435?" the woman's voice repeated in my ear. She sounded almost jovial. "Please nod if this is your number."

What the hell? The number was very familiar. Then I remembered. It was the library card I'd used while I was going to the Université de Montréal. It was my number!

I nodded.

And that's when all hell broke loose.

Twenty-Five

A SYMBOL FOR WISDOM

BY ALL HELL, I mean a *thuck* and a *thwuck* and a *thwack*. The pressure on my arm was relieved, and the vampire fell across me, knocking the last minuscule bit of air out of my lungs. There was a dart sticking out of her neck. I lifted my head to see Patty dashing across the room, dodging what looked like white puffs of smoke smashing on boxes, wooden beams and crates near her. Each puff had a corresponding *thuck* and *thwuck* and *thwack*. But none of the projectiles found a home in Patty. As she jumped through the rear window, the last *thwuck* caught her in the shoulder, and she tumbled out onto the street.

Something—or someone—landed softly next to me, and I turned my head and tried to get up. But my arm was weak, and I was dizzy from the gas and from having my head slammed into the cement several times and also from my ribs being kicked several hundred times. I was truly pooched, because I'd begun hallucinating—the woman

BETRAYAL

looking down at me was in a multicolored ninja suit, her bright-blue eyes cold as steel. I could see right through her to the ceiling above me.

That made no sense at all.

Her lips were moving, but I couldn't hear her words. Another ninja landed beside her, and then a third. They were both in white outfits, clutching crossbows. The nearest one had an icon of a book on her shoulder.

A book! A symbol of wisdom. What the hell did that mean?

Blue Eyes' lips moved again, and the words came through my fog. "What happened to the primary target?"

"Evaded capture," the second white ninja said.

"Black-bag those bodies." She pointed across the storage space, then gestured down at me. "And green-bag this one." Did she think I was dead?

But then the woman was lifted off me. It was as if a truck had been pulled from my shoulders.

"Who are you?" I said. Though it came out like *Wooru?*

The multicolored ninja reached down and touched my forehead gently. I could still see parts of the room through her. She pulled off a multicolored glove and set a bare hand on my neck. At first I thought it was a choke hold because, well, I'm trained to think that way. But she was pressing against my carotid, taking my pulse. My heartbeat thumped against her finger.

"We're the Returns Team," she said, as if it explained everything.

"Oh."

"You're Amber Fang, correct?"

I did my best to nod. Though I believe I only managed a blink or two.

"Well, you're going to sleep now, Amber. But don't worry, you're among friends. Really good friends. There are things you shouldn't see, though, so we're sending you to Neverland."

"But," I said. Which was all the argument I could come up with. There was a pinprick in my shoulder, and, as she had promised me, I fell toward Neverland.

Sleep didn't come right away though. I was lifted by four white ninjas, and I tried my damnedest to keep my eyes open. I glimpsed another ninja zipping Hexdall into a black body bag. They were doing the same with another one of the vampires. The vampire who had fallen on me was in a green bag with airholes. Then they carried me toward the doors.

Blink.

Now I was outside. There was a white van that said *Bookmobile* on the side.

Blink.

Bookmobile?

I was inside the vehicle, lying on a stretcher. There was a row of books along one wall. Crossbows, gas masks and sniper rifles hung on the other.

Blink.

A white ninja was looking down at me. "She's still awake."

"Another dose," the see-through ninja said. Her voice had the tone of authority. Now I could see the row of books right through her. How was that possible?

I couldn't open my mouth to protest. I did manage to lift a finger.

There was another pinprick in my opposite shoulder.

"Sleep, Amber," she commanded gently. "Really, you need to sleep."

And, as if she also had command of that, I slept.

I dreamed of Peter Pan.

Twenty-Six
OF BIBLIOBURROS AND BEYOND

BOOKMOBILE.

The word was stuck in my head. I couldn't wake up, even though I'd long stopped dreaming about Peter Pan and Neverland. My mind was aware enough that it kept singling out that one word: *bookmobile*. I know the history of those great biblio vehicles inside and out. It is a particular infatuation of mine. One of the first bookmobiles was called the Warrington Perambulating Library, a one-horse van that brought books to the residents of Cheshire, England. The unfortunately named Mary Lemist Titcomb (I mean, is Lemist even a name?) had a fancy two-horse bookmobile that she used to enlighten the rural residents of Washington County, Maryland. Eventually bookmobiles became Model Ts, vans and modern-day buses.

But my favorite bookmobile by far is the Biblioburro, a traveling library that is carried by two donkeys (along with teacher Luis Soriano) to bring books to kids in rural villages

BETRAYAL

near La Gloria, Colombia. Proof that you can learn from an ass. Or two.

I could hear the low rumbling of a motor, and occasionally we hit a bump. I was in a bookmobile, and that vehicle contained both books and white ninjas. I was beginning to question my sanity.

There was weight on every part of my body, as if one of those lead X-ray–blocking blankets had been laid across me. I knew it was the drug in my system causing the sensation. I still couldn't open my eyes, and my companions were as silent as a shushed library.

The movement eventually stopped. Now I heard whispering, and it suddenly felt as though a hundred caterpillars had crawled underneath me. The caterpillars carried me toward where I thought the door was. I was exiting the bookmobile. Cool air caressed my forehead. A bird chirped. And I wondered if I was in the woods. There was some brightness in my face.

I managed to creak an eyelid open.

Four of the white ninjas were carrying me. I'm not heavy, so they made it look easy. The multicolored ninja was still see-through. Behind her was a brick wall with a layer of green climbing vines. The whole country of England was just one big green thumb. I had the impression we were in a very small park, surrounded by brick walls on both sides.

My eyelid thudded closed.

When I creaked it open a second time, I was still floating through the cottage-like greenery. A lone tree loomed above

ARTHUR SLADE

us, and we passed a sundial and a white bench. Then my eye shut again. The sound of a door opening got me to open both eyes to discover we were now inside the brick building, having just gone through a thick door.

"She's waking up," one of the ninjas said. They all had female shapes.

"You'll have to work on your doses, Agnes," the multi-colored one answered.

There was a sign on the wall that said *Bromley House Library*. We passed near a spiral staircase and shelves of books. There was bright light, almost too bright for me to take, coming in the windows. I closed my eyes.

Yes, I tried to say. *I'm awake*. But my lips wouldn't move.

A period of darkness followed. Then I was being jostled slightly, and I slowly became aware that I was being set on a hard surface. I creaked open my eyes again to see that I was on a table in a room with an unlit fireplace. They had moved several fancy wooden chairs away from the table (the chairs had carved tops that mimicked castle battlements). The place smelled of old books and old knowledge. It was a relaxing smell.

"The library is closed to members right now," the see-through ninja said. She patted my shoulder as if she had just explained everything. "We're going to look after your wounds. You are with friends."

That lead-blanket sensation hadn't left my body. The ninjas were friendly. I made that assumption since they hadn't killed me and had killed, or at least incapaci-tated, my attackers, though I couldn't quite remember if

BETRAYAL

Patty had gotten away—only that she'd broken a window and landed outside.

"Whr m I?" I slurred.

She gestured around her. One hand was gloveless, but I could still see through the rest of her. It was so odd. "Bromley House Library, Nottingham. It's a safe house. Well, a safe library. All of them are, of course, to a certain degree."

The little map of England in my head helped me to calculate that we'd traveled about a hundred miles north of Oxford. I was pretty certain the ninjas were all female, judging by their size and body shapes, though there were a few thicker-set ones that could be male. It was more their eyebrows that told me they were likely female. One ninja was working on my hand. I felt a sharp poke there. "Sorry, I should have warned you." She really did look contrite. She'd lowered her ninja mask, and her dark-skinned face showed contrition. "It's freezing. Your stitches have torn."

"Agnes is good at stitching together old books. Oh, and wounds," the head ninja said.

I was still a bundle of lethargy and couldn't have put up a fight if I'd wanted to. It was clearly a combination of the drugs they'd hit me with, the smoke Hexdall had used (I still didn't know what to think of his heroic action) and general exhaustion.

"Who are you?" I asked.

"We're your friends, Amber," the see-through ninja said. "And we're librarians."

I wasn't used to librarians looking so lethal. Well, except at the information desk when you asked for something stupid.

"You're hard to look at," I said.

Her eyebrows contorted, and then she let out a hoarse chuckle. "Oh yes, the invisibility cloak. I'll shut it off." She hit herself in the collarbone, and her outfit went all white. "There, that's better. How unprofessional of me."

"We were making a bet to see how long before you noticed," Agnes said. "I won two Dickens. Originals, of course."

There was more laughter. Had they just bet using rare books? What sort of people were they?

"To answer your question," the woman said, "we call ourselves the Returns." She removed her face cowl. She appeared to be in her late forties and had hard, intelligent, blue eyes. "I'm Theressa Dane. A metadata analyst and all-round fun human."

An epoch passed before I could come up with something to say. "But really, who are you? What is this? I'm starting to freak out."

"The Returns, well, you don't know this yet, but we are the keepers of knowledge. We are the defenders of humanity's arts and sciences and history."

"She makes it sound so noble and grand," someone said from the corner of the room. More gentle laughter followed.

"Ignore the cacklers. The cracksters. The crones. We're the secret organization that has members in every library in the world."

"Are you the Illuminati?" I asked.

"Ha! No. In fact, there's no such thing. Anyway, we wanted to call ourselves the Dewey Do Gooders, but there was too

BETRAYAL

much infighting with Library of Congress Classification system supporters." She put up her hands. "Anyway, don't get me going on that old argument. We are officially the Preservational Librarians Guild. The preserves—get it?"

"It's a very jammy pun," one of the ninjas shouted. Obviously, it was an old joke.

I didn't react to the humor. I really didn't get it. "Oh, jam," I said a moment later.

"Yes, well, our sense of humor grows on you," Theressa admitted. "Our PLG team is called the Returns Team, the Returns for short."

"The Returns?"

She nodded. "When all of society falls apart, or parts of it do, we will return it. To the way it was. Of course, you also get the reference to book returns, right? Let's just say we're proactive about returns. When the Preservational Librarians Guild needs us to reach out and touch someone, we do. Every country has a secret chapter of the PLG. Every library branch has a connection."

"But—but what is your purpose?" I asked.

"To save the world." This got gales of laughter from the other ninjas.

"Are you real ninjas?"

"No. We've studied and trained in proper ninjutsu though. The library branches in Japan are where we train. And, of course, there are ninjutsu libraries. It's only natural that their knowledge would be disseminated and enlisted to help our cause."

ARTHUR SLADE

"Oh." I wasn't coming up with much. I'll blame it on the drugs. "So you're librarians?"

"Yes, you're getting the basic concept."

"And you just want to save the world." More laughter erupted from the ninja gallery.

"Technically, our prime directive is to preserve human knowledge and civilization. We're just a bit more proactive than the majority of the library systems."

There was, apparently, no part of my body that didn't hurt. But I managed to keep my mind in the game. "And why did you rescue me?"

"You're one of us. We have been watching your metadata since you got your first library card."

"Isn't that against privacy rules?"

"It's all in how you interpret it." Theressa said this without blushing. "Like I said, we're proactive."

"How did you even know I was in England? It's not like I checked out any books."

"Remember the electronic terminal in Heathrow Airport?" she asked.

"Yes." I had been the 1066th person to use it.

"We got your fingerprints from there. And again from a kiosk in the hotel lobby."

"But—but that's a total invasion of privacy!"

"Like I said, we're a little more proactive than other libraries." She brushed some dust off her ninja suit. "And you'd be dead right now if we were less proactive."

BETRAYAL

I couldn't argue with that. Actually, I could. "Well, they were only going to take out my ovaries. But I don't think I'd have survived long after that."

Theressa nodded. "You are a bit of a star in the field."

"I am?"

"Yeah, we don't have many vampire librarians. Well, just you, actually. And you have followers. Fans, actually—Fangers, they call themselves."

Fangers? WTF? "So how do you know that I'm the only vampire librarian?"

"We reached out to other vampires and even to the Grand Council."

"You did?" I couldn't imagine how. A librarian/vampire conference?

"Yes, but they weren't so friendly. It led to the loss of two senior librarians and a page."

"I'm sorry."

"All three of them are on the memorial wall," she said. It sounded like a great honor, and she seemed to believe that somehow the dead would be satisfied with that.

"What are you going to do with Hexdall and the others you bagged?" I asked.

"Agent Hexdall will be cremated and sent to one of the League locations that we have identified. The dead vampires will also be cremated and buried in an unmarked mausoleum. The live ones are part of our catch-and-release program."

"You let them go!"

ARTHUR SLADE

"Yes." She raised a hand. "I understand your concern, but we don't like to interfere with the natural order of things. We preserve."

"But—but they kill people. Humans!"

"You kill people," she pointed out.

"I mean, they kill anyone. I only feed on murderers."

"We preserve all knowledge. All societies. It's not our place to exterminate or imprison members of a society, even a vampire society. We stepped in to save you because you are one of our own."

There was a whole bunch of moralizing and mind bending I'd have to unpack to fully understand their ideals. And I didn't have the brainpower at that moment. "So what are you going to do with me?"

"You're part of our catch-and-release program too. I, of course, can't resist telling you to study harder. But you can leave whenever you want."

"Is there, like, a Returns signal if I need help?"

"No. There isn't. But we could give you a card that allows us to track you more directly."

I thought of the tracker the League had inserted in me. I hated that horrible sense of always being watched. It was the opposite of how my mother had raised me. "No," I said. "No, thanks."

"We understand. Just remember, every library is a safe place. You can always go there if you're in trouble."

I nodded. Then a thought struck me. An obvious thought. "I have a request. A requisition."

BETRAYAL

"Yes."

"I'm trying to find my mother."

"We know." They knew too much. Far too much. But I asked my question anyway.

"Do...do you have anything on her? Any metadata? Do you know where she is?"

"We can't help you with that."

I took a second to process this. "Does that mean you don't know or you won't tell me?"

"You mother rarely used the library system."

"You still haven't answered my question." There was a hint of testiness in my voice.

"We can't help you. If we have the answer, we can't access it."

"Who can access it?"

"The higher-ups. The library board." Again, this was said as if it answered everything.

"Then you're no help to me." I regretted saying that almost immediately. And I wasn't good at dealing with regret. Mom had taught me better manners than this. "Thank you, I meant to say."

"You've been looking for a long time." She said it with sympathy and patted my left hand at the same time. The last vestiges of my anger melted.

"Yes, I have."

"We will take care of you anytime. What do you want now?"

"I should rest. And contact my partner and—" My rumbling stomach interrupted me. "I have one more request. An odd one. Do you understand my requirements for food?"

"Yes. You have a moral code for your sustenance. Many are the articles we've written about your feeding patterns. They're on the librarians' dark web."

There was a librarians' dark web? "That's an honor. How do I get a pass card for your dark web?"

"Someday, Amber. Just complete your studies."

"Yes, well, back to me eating. With all the metadata at your fingertips, can you find me a meal?"

"Yes." She said this without hesitation.

"And it will be…" I looked for the right way to express my concerns. "Morally kosher?"

"You have my word."

I nearly hugged her.

"Within the next twelve hours, you will receive a text with an address and a name," Theressa said. "We have a hotel to send you to. It's safe, secure and quiet. You can wait there while you recuperate."

"Then take me to the hotel."

I said goodbye to Theressa, and Agnes finished dressing my wound. Two other ninjas, now in ordinary street dress and looking properly librarianish, brought clothes for me, which were very much my own style. Agnes helped me dress, not an easy task since every bone felt broken.

Twenty minutes later they walked me to the front door. A bookmobile was waiting. My fellow librarians helped me out to the street, which was ironically called Angel Row. They got me onto a mattress surrounded by books. Agnes shook my hand for an extra-long time. Maybe she was a Fanger. "Not everyone agrees we should be so passive," she whispered. Then she said more loudly, "Good luck on all fronts, Amber Fang."

She backed out and closed the door.

I lay on the mattress, and the bookmobile began to move ahead. "We're on our way," the driver said. She had a thick accent.

Only then did I realize that Agnes had left something in my hand.

A note.

It said: *Information should be shared. Your mother's last known address is this.*

The remainder of the note consisted of the words *access point* followed by a series of coordinates.

I glowed. A lead. A solid lead after years of searching.

I put the note in my breast pocket. And then, surprisingly, I fell asleep.

Twenty-Seven
WALLOWING IN THE WELLOW

THE WELLOW IS A BRICK HOTEL in Grimsby, a city on the east coast of England. The air holds the salty spray smell of the Humber estuary just across the road. My limited memory reminded me that the estuary led to the North Sea (my time perusing Dewey Decimal section 900, Geography and History, was paying off). Another odd fact stuck in my think-box: people from Grimsby are called Grimbarians. A life of reading anything and everything I could get my hands on has led to an odd collection of data.

The hotel provided bangers and mash for breakfast, which I skipped. I slept the entire day, and when I woke up I was thinking about Hexdall. He didn't have to try to rescue me, yet he had. The man had guts and a heart. And I wished, belatedly, I'd been more kind to him. My decision to try to get Patty on my own had inadvertently led to his death (though I found some slight comfort in the fact that he'd made his own choice to join the fight and, of course, he'd chosen this dangerous type of employment). I'd miss him, I decided. And the next time I saw Dermot, I promised myself I'd try to learn everything I could about Hexdall. So I could remember the real man. Not just my first grumpy impressions of him.

My phone buzzed. I opened it and discovered a text from *Anonymous* that said **Joe Blight**. The next two lines were an address in North Thoresby, a nearby village, and below that was the image of a man in his early thirties with a plain face and glasses. Obviously, this was from the Returns. Only one day was left before I *had* to eat. I'd have to go out for dinner now. If there was anyone in the world I could trust with information, it had to be librarians. Even ones who called themselves the Preservational Librarians Guild.

That said, I still looked up Joe Blight online and discovered that his supervisor at the local post office had been murdered. Joe Blight was detained as a person of interest but was later released. I was pretty sure I knew why he'd ended up on the PLG's list of moral murders.

I texted Dermot: **Hi D. Will call after dinner.**

Then I went out and hunted down my prey. North Thoresby was a small village with a large brick church as its centerpiece. Joe lived in a red brick house surrounded by other red brick houses. I'm sure it was safe against the big bad wolf, but not against me. When I went in through the bathroom window, I could hear three heartbeats. A little bit of creeping around let me know that Joe was living with his parents. Yet another thirty-year-old who'd moved back home.

I ate him, but I didn't leave a mess—not one red drop of blood—just in case his parents were nice folks with a bad child. Joe would look like he'd died of natural causes. Well, except for the extreme paleness.

I discovered that British blood doesn't have a specific taste. Though it was clear that Joe had had a few pints that evening. Several pounds heavier, I slunk back to the hotel and slept.

When I awoke it was dark. I'd been out for almost twenty-four more hours. My hand was itching again, but not painfully so. And my other bruises were retreating. I knew if I looked in the mirror, my cheeks would be back to their pale selves.

I was fed. I had my mother's last known address. And my life felt like it was coming together.

I realized I couldn't quite picture Mom's face. It had been three years. I'd know her face if I ever saw it again, but when my apartment in Montreal had blown up, I'd lost my only photo of her. I missed looking at her. She'd never signed up for Facebook, of course, or Myspace, and she purposefully had no presence on the internet. What if I forgot what she looked like entirely?

I ached to have her hand on my shoulder. I ached to hug her.

My phone buzzed with a text: **ARE YOU THERE?**

Dermot was waiting at the other end of the world. I had meant to contact him when I got back to the hotel, but sleep had won over my previous promise to him. I dialed the number programmed into my phone.

BETRAYAL

"Amber," he said. Maybe he had a particular ringtone for me. Angelic bells? There was a gentle, tired tone to his voice. I must say a very minor melt began in my heart. Or it was a bleed.

"Yes. It's me. Reporting in." My voice reflected my own tiredness.

"It's good to hear you. I have been worried. Tell me what happened."

"Hexdall is dead." It was actually quite hard to say.

"Yes. I'm aware of that. His ashes appeared here yesterday."

"Already?"

"Yes. A bike courier dropped them off. I couldn't trace the original source of the delivery. And I immediately packed up and went to a different safe house. One day I'll take Hexdall to the League mausoleum. Can you explain what happened?"

Where to start? I told him everything from the moment we landed in Heathrow until now. Except I skipped the part about knowing my mother's latest whereabouts. I thought my story made sense, but I couldn't be certain. I was feeling mushy and mushed. I ended the whole tale with, "I liked Hexdall in the end."

"He was a good man," Dermot said.

"Yes. He was."

Silence. "What did you think of these librarians?" he asked. "I haven't had the slightest whiff of intel on an organization like that. I would almost accuse you of imagining things. It seems rather odd that they exist."

"It's not much odder than an organization called the League dedicated to ridding the world of bad guys and gals." There was a bit of defensiveness in my voice.

"*Touché*," he said rather quietly. "But we're not much of an organization these days."

"Don't be a Debbie Downer." I kept the sarcasm out of my voice. "How are you?"

"You wouldn't recognize me. I'm like that character in that Stephen King book *Thinner*."

"Did you just make a literary reference?" I pulled the phone away from my ear, stared at it for a moment in shock, then put it back. "You should get a star on your paper for that."

"The desiccation has slowed. But I think the only thing that has saved me is my augmentations."

"Can the effects be reversed?"

"It doesn't look promising."

I swallowed. "What are you going to do?"

"Kill her," he said.

"Take a number. But I meant, what are you going to do about your health?"

"That's between me and my doctor."

"Really, Dermot, tell me."

"No." He was abrupt, which was not like him at all. There was a long pause before he spoke. "What are your intentions now?"

"I want to track my sister down. And find my mother. And maybe my father. Oh, and kill that AI. And—"

"That's a long list. In what order would you like to do that?"

BETRAYAL

"Mom," I said. "I want to see my mom first."

"Do you still want our help?"

"Yes. " It surprised me that I didn't hesitate. "Listen, am I talking to you? Or to the League?"

"I am the League. I haven't found a single member of the board alive. There are a few cells and ground teams remaining. But, for all intents and purposes, I am the League. So you're talking to both at once."

"Well, I only want to share this information with you," I said. Trust is not my middle name.

"You're talking to me, Amber. Just me."

I took a deep breath. "One of the librarians gave me my mother's last known address. Well, she called it an access point."

He went silent again. Was he weighing what this all meant?

"Then we'll get her, Amber. You and I. We'll find your mother, and then we will figure out what to do with what remains of the League. Perhaps this will be the League's last mission. I'll send for you. Just wait in your current location, and I'll bring you to this safe house."

So I hung up and waited. Six hours later a black car showed up outside the Wellow and I stepped into the open back door, crossing my fingers that I really was on my way to find my mother.

Twenty-Eight
BEHIND ALL THAT CLUNKING

I HOPPED A BRITISH AIRWAYS FLIGHT to Houston using the identity the driver had given me. I didn't touch a single library terminal in Heathrow. Partway through the flight, I went to the washroom and removed the stitches that Agnes, the librarian ninja (how I laugh at those two words being together), had sewn into me. My hand was perfectly healed, though there would be a small scar. I opened and closed it several times, thanking my vampire genetics for the ability to heal quickly. I left the stitches in the garbage and returned to my seat to watch another movie.

I grew bored of the next movie and sunk my teeth into *The Girl on the Train*. After almost a hundred pages, we began to descend. The George Bush Intercontinental Airport is not the most attractive structure, but it has a lot of windows and exterior light going for it. It also had an overabundant share of middle-aged men and women in short-sleeved shirts and khaki shorts. Humanity looked so different to me when I wasn't hungry. They no longer looked like fully dressed hot dogs.

BETRAYAL

A black car picked me up at the airport. Just once I'd like to see a mauve or indigo secret-agent vehicle. Lime green would be sublime. The car took me through the bowels of Houston to what looked to be a factory section near the various docks and waterways of the city. We passed several ExxonMobil sites that I guessed were oil refineries—the tall metal towers leaking flame looked both futuristic and apocalyptic at the same time. We pulled into a deserted collection of hangars and stopped in front of an old bar called Satan's Head that had maybe been popular in the 1980s.

The door to the car opened on its own, and the driver grunted, "Good luck." I got out, and the car pulled away. The idea of meeting Dermot in a bar with such a tough-sounding name almost made me chuckle. I walked up, creaked open the front door and went into a large square-shaped bar. It smelled like the place had been dead for ten years. In fact, the stink was strong enough to suggest a few of the patrons might have died and been left under the floorboards.

My reflection looked back at me from the mirror behind the bar. There was broken glass scattered across one section of the floor.

Then came a clunk, clunk, clunk.

I did hear a faint heartbeat behind it, but mostly my sensitive ears picked up whirring. And my mind, which so easily will jump down the rabbit hole of paranoia, said, *It's a trap! A trap!* Funny—I sound like Mom when I think things like that.

But I didn't listen to that voice. I was pretty certain I knew what was going on. The door behind the bar opened, and a stranger walked toward me—a thin man encased in an exoskeleton.

"Would you like something to drink, Amber?" Dermot asked. He was almost unrecognizable, except for the cleft chin and the clear gray eyes. I'd not seen him for a week, and I guessed he'd lost nearly eighty pounds. He also hadn't shaved in that time. His beginning of a beard looked gray.

"You look so different," I said. I couldn't make it sound cheery.

"I'll take that as a compliment." His arm whirred as he leaned against the bar. "I've atrophied 30 percent, losing weight and muscle mass. Even my organs are shrinking. But, and I know you'll argue with this, I haven't lost any brain mass. Your sister's paralytic agent is extremely potent. I much prefer yours."

"I'm so sorry you're going through this," I said. If only I'd known the damage she'd cause, I'd have left her back in Antarctica as a frozen couch for the penguins.

"Well, your tone suggests you think I'm on death's door. Really, I'm not. I'm not."

He was a step away from death's door, at the very least, but there was a light in his eyes. And anger. I had to remember that he'd just lost a friend, Hexdall, and many other comrades and co-workers had been killed when the League was attacked. All the stress was obviously weighing on him too.

Something about his new thin and sallow look gave a Victorian tinge to his appearance. It was almost handsome. Well, not Mr. Darcy handsome, but that is a high bar for any male.

BETRAYAL

Of course, the exoskeleton gave Dermot's appearance a steampunk vibe.

He did pour himself a drink without smashing the glass and then added water to the rum. His metal fingertips clinked the whole time. "I did find a bottle of red wine," he said. He brought it up from a hidden cupboard in the bar. "Nineteen eighty. A good year."

I nodded, and he poured me a glass. I took a long sip. It was actually quite passable. Wine is the closest thing to blood that I enjoy drinking. "Give me a 1980 wine and an 1880 book, and I'm in heaven," I said.

That got a smile out of him. His teeth were bright white, the healthiest part of him. "You are such an interesting ball of contradictions."

"Well, don't be afraid to bounce this ball." God, that sounded stupid. Obviously, I was still tired. And confused about why I found him so attractive in this vulnerable state. Was it some sort of horrible motherly instinct?

Compassion? Nah!

He was too busy watching my right hand to notice my momentary discomfort. "Your hand has healed."

"Mostly." I flexed my fingers. "I took the stitches out in the airplane. There's a nice scar." I made a fist and imagined smashing it into my sister's nose. Then I sipped more of the wine. The second mouthful was divine.

"So," he said, pausing for a long enough time that I thought he'd passed out with his eyes open. "I have a plan. And I want your approval."

"I'm all ears."

"I am certain it's ZARC that attempted to wipe out the League." I didn't want to say that it was more than an attempt. Was it possible to have a League with only one person? "And since Patty and the vampires are searching for your mother, then she's most likely imprisoned by ZARC. That indicates that the coordinates you have are for a ZARC compound of some sort."

"That all makes sense to me."

"Well, our purposes dovetail. You want your mother. I want to gather more data about their organization. And maybe just poke them in the eye." The last sentence was said rather harshly. "I am wondering whether this Hector Artificial Intelligence actually runs the organization as a kind of electronic overseer—a secretary for Anthony Zarc. Hector is obviously a human-level AI, and everything I've read says we're twenty years away from that. If he doesn't control the organization but does the mental grunt work, then that's interesting too. How do they control him? Do they have some sort of lock on Hector? It could be as simple as an explosive device on his main hard drive." He waved his metal hands. "Anyway, it's all very theoretical. He exists. I assume Anthony Zarc has a means of controlling him. And we must find a way to get to the heart of their organization."

"So we start by finding and rescuing my mother. I'm game for that."

"Good. Good. I'll set up a team. I have a few favors to call in and a few bank accounts to drain. Our primary goal is to

BETRAYAL

extract your mother and gather intel. And when we return with your mother, you'll owe me."

"Owe you?" My tone of voice showed that I didn't like the sound of that.

"Yeah, a drink at least," he said.

"Are you asking me out on a date?"

He blushed. He was a hardened man, trained to be a secret agent, and he still blushed.

Sometimes I thought he was just a great big kid inside.

Twenty-Nine
PASSING THE LAST OUTPOST

THE FLIGHT TO CANADA took us to Winnipeg, and then we got on another plane that spat us out in a city with the mysterious name of Saskatoon, Saskatchewan. Where the Canadians came up with these names was anyone's guess. Maybe all their naming decisions happened after a hockey concussion.

We loaded into a six-seater twin-prop plane and began on our way to a northern hunting lodge. By *we* I mean there were four of us. Dermot was there, of course, and he moved slowly because he'd stashed his exoskeleton in a large suitcase. He did look a bit better though. He had to use a cane, and I found myself taking his arm several times. My remaining two companions were both Chinese people, one male, one female. They had appeared on the tarmac of the Saskatoon John G. Diefenbaker International Airport. As far as I could tell, they were mute. At least, they only nodded when we were introduced.

We were supposed to be passing as a rich businessman (Dermot), his wife (me) and our assistants. And we were

BETRAYAL

heading north to hunt big game—black bears, specifically. I pretended to be excited about that. I don't hunt for sport. Only for food. And so it took a bit of acting on my part.

We flew across flat, stark prairies with dots of sloughs and small lakes here and there. It was the middle of March, and snow still whitened the ground. Only a few patches of bare earth showed through. Within an hour or so we encountered a line of forest that became the norm for the remainder of the flight. There was the occasional lake, but generally it was trees, trees and more pine trees. I listened to the buzzing sound of the engine, expecting it to quit at any time.

"Uh, does this thing have pontoons?" I asked.

"The wheels stay retracted," the pilot said. He had a southern accent, which sounded odd this far north. "The Gweduck is designed to land on its belly, ma'am." I was slightly offended at being called a ma'am. It…well, it sounds so old. I was tapping my fingers on my knee somewhat frantically. I'd read far too many stories of crashes in the forest and people having to eat the survivors. Dermot didn't look like much more than a morsel. "I built the plane from a kit," the pilot added proudly.

I gripped the seat tightly now, cutting into the fabric, then doubled that pressure when a bank of clouds moved in. It was like flying through a cigar lounge.

"That's La Loche down there," the pilot said as the clouds broke briefly, revealing a small town. Perhaps *La Loche* is French for "the last outpost." Farther and farther we buzzed into the clouds.

ARTHUR SLADE

Finally he brought us under the cloud cover and aimed straight for what looked to be a green ocean of trees. As far as I could tell, the pilot had gone all kamikaze. He nearly brushed the tops of several pine trees, and then a lake appeared in front of us. We scooted down and hopped, skidded and slid across the water, the impact hard enough that I reached across to stop Dermot from smashing his nose.

We eventually puttered up to a wooden dock that looked like it had been built pre-World War II. The pilot gave a jaunty wave, then sat back in the seat of his plane and started reading *A Storm of Swords*. So that's how he'd pass his time waiting for us. He had grown in my estimation. If we had time, I decided I would ask his opinions on the red wedding scene.

I grabbed my backpack, and as I reached to pick up Dermot's huge suitcase, one of our companions latched onto it and lugged it easily down the dock. We walked into the woods, heading south. Occasionally Dermot checked his watch, which I assumed had some sort of compass on it. Then he pulled out an actual compass.

"Going all Boy Scout, are you?"

He nodded but didn't answer. He wasn't moving as fast as I'd have liked to see, and his breathing was rather shallow.

"So where did you find our two friends?"

"Ask them," Dermot said. "They speak English."

"Oh," I said. Ugh, I really should have been more careful. "So what part of China are you from?"

"I'm from Philly," the woman said gruffly.

"And I'm from Paris," said the man. "Paris, Texas, of course."

BETRAYAL

I nearly slapped myself in the head. Why would I make such an idiotic assumption? I was a librarian. I'd lived in North America all my life and knew firsthand about the variety of ethnic backgrounds. On top of that, I'd consumed people of all shapes and sizes and ethnicities. I should have known better!

"Um, what are your names?" I asked, realizing Dermot hadn't told me their names when we first met.

"I'm Derek," the man said.

"I'm Steph," the woman said.

And that was the end of the conversation. I totally got why they wouldn't want to talk to me any longer.

We walked. Hours ticked by. So did the evergreens. The bush was thick, and the path we followed must have been made made by deer or bears—I hoped the former. The cold worked its way through my coat and into my flesh.

"How much farther do we have to go?" I asked finally. I tried not to sound like a bored child on a car ride.

"We wanted to land far enough away that they wouldn't hear the plane," Dermot said. "So we have a jaunt."

"Couldn't we have just flown in on gliders? I hear they're quiet."

"Have you ever piloted a glider?" he asked.

"No."

"Then that's why. Plus, flying into a forested area isn't wise when you aren't motorized."

Well, skinny and sick as he was, Dermot could still be extremely aggravating.

The cold continued to settle into my bones. Dermot was moving even slower. He did pause to pat something on his shoulder, which I realized must be some sort of medical pick-me-up because his pace immediately improved.

A few minutes later, without a signal that I would have noticed, Derek ran ahead into the bush, moving quickly but without even snapping a branch. He returned ten minutes later and made a sharp hand signal to Dermot, and we got down and crawled ahead. The forest floor was not welcoming. The pine needles and squirrel poop were not something I remembered from all the action films I'd watched.

Eventually we stopped at the edge of a clearing. I nearly did a double take.

We were looking at a moon base.

Thirty
SOS

THERE WERE CONCRETE containment walls that looked to be higher than the Great Wall of China. Beyond that were several bunker-like buildings and tall cylinder shapes. A rusted dump truck that looked like it'd been left by a giant sat at the edge of one wall. Beside that was a long line of ATCO trailers for workers. And on the side of a concrete tower in the middle of the compound was a symbol. *SOS*.

"What does that stand for?" I whispered.

"Saskatchewan Oil Sands," Dermot said, doing his best impression of Google. "This was home base for a now-defunct oil sands company. I did my research on the way up."

"Not the best name."

"It sticks in the head. Perhaps that's all that matters."

"Well, it was bad luck for them."

I guessed, by the undergrowth, that the compound had been abandoned a few years earlier. If my memory of the news cycle was correct, that was about the same time OPEC turned on the oil taps, killing so many oil businesses across North America. Sometime after that, ZARC had moved in.

"So do we have a more specific plan?" I asked.

"I needed to see it up close," Dermot said. "We're going to wait until after midnight, and then you can sneak in and poke around."

"That's your plan?"

"When you have someone as versatile and talented as you, one doesn't need much more than that. We'll provide backup."

It was my turn to blush. Whether he meant it or not, I couldn't help but be excited by the compliment.

We waited. Darkness came as it always does, though this far north and with all the tree cover, it felt as if the sun just fell away in the blink of an eye. Lights came on in the compound, lighting up the ground around several of the buildings. The trailers were mostly dark, which suggested to me a small population of workers. The fewer the better. No one came outside, and there were no noticeable patrols. I doubted they had skimped on security, since they were an arms dealer, so they obviously had other means of patrolling and protecting their grounds. The slight buzz of drones tickled my ears, and I took a moment to source them. Five in total were within hearing distance.

We waited until after midnight. It may have been the witching hour, but it was also most likely that most of the inhabitants would be asleep by then.

"Here," Dermot whispered, "put these on." He handed me a subvocal mic, an earbud and a tiny camera that clipped over my ear. "It's so I can watch what's going on inside. I'll be right beside you the whole time."

"And half a mile away at the same time," I said. I put the devices on. They were impressively light. The camera wasn't much heavier than an earring.

I stripped off my coat, despite the chill. I was wearing a black special-ops suit that Dermot had dug up for me. It was thin, though, and I hoped my movements would give me enough heat. The rustling of a winter jacket could sound like thunder when you were trying to sneak up on someone. I had fingerless gloves on too. I stood up. My legs nearly cramped, and I took a half minute to stretch out. There were still far too many aches and pains to list from the beating I'd taken.

"Toodles," I said.

"Amber." Dermot's voice was heavy. "Don't do anything crazy."

"Crazy? That suggests I've done crazy in the past."

"The past speaks for itself. But I know you can get emotional sometimes."

"I don't!"

Derek and Steph both watched us carefully. It was dark, but I was pretty sure I saw consternation on their faces.

"Just remember," Dermot said. "We need to look before we leap."

"You're very gifted at aphorisms. But I'm just going to go in, look around and sneak back out. I promise, Dermot." I tapped the camera. "It will be the most boring documentary on the planet."

ARTHUR SLADE

"Good, keep it boring. And take care, okay?"

"I will." Then I was off. I didn't make a beeline for the main building but walked to the nearest fallen structure. As far as my eyes and ears told me, there were no heartbeats or infrared beams. I could guesstimate the location of the drones from the sound of their rotors. The suit should hide me from their heat sensors. I hugged concrete, sliding along the shadows.

When I was about one hundred yards from the main building, the first heartbeats *thumped* into my awareness, and I caught the scent of humans. Adrenaline began running through my system. It was always tricky to stop it from over-powering my focus. But I'd been hunting for a long time.

"There's a guard on your left," Dermot said into my ear. "I'm sure you've seen him."

"I have," I subvocalized. I hadn't seen the damn guard, but I did now. There was a man in black-and-gray khaki on one of the roofs. I should have separated his heartbeat from the others, but there was a cluster in the building below him. I kept myself out of the guard's line of vision.

It was becoming difficult to keep track of the drones, the guard and the various heartbeats. I walked as lightly as possible, in case there were mines or movement sensors, and slowly worked my way up to the main concrete building. The windows were covered with mesh wire, perhaps to keep bears out. Well, removing it would be too loud, so it'd keep vampires out too. I scaled the wall, peeked over the top, saw nothing and stole onto the roof.

BETRAYAL

"Good work," Dermot said.

"I don't need a cheerleader," I subvocalized. I meant it to sound somewhat lighthearted, but I didn't know if subvocalized words could express sarcasm. Well, he was big boy— he'd have to deal with it. I had other things on my to-do list, like how to get into the building. There were several vents, each with wire mesh across them. But these were designed to keep birds out, so I was able to quietly snap the wire and bend it away from the largest vent. I climbed in face first. For all I knew, this vent could send me right into a furnace, and I'd be Kentucky Fried Amber. But you didn't spend your life slipping in and out of tight places without getting a knack for it. The air coming out wasn't too warm. And I did smell a bit of meat cooking and the not-so-pleasant off-venting of a washroom. Down the vent I went, Alice in Wonderland with fangs.

There is a trick to squirming through ducts without squeaking or creaking, and it involves putting pressure on all sides of the metal at once. I squiggled left after about fifteen feet. The building was rectangular, and there wasn't any easy way to know where I was, other than my old trick of listening to heartbeats. I did come across a grill and saw a hallway below and a security guard in black-and-gray fatigues walking nearby. Why couldn't these people pump some color into their wardrobes?

I took another left and caught that freshly disgusting bathroom scent. That was a room I could come down into, but it was most likely occupied. People, even dark, evil gun-runner types, like to avoid work by hanging out on the toilet. They need to check their Facebook statuses somewhere. So I crept along until I found a dark room below me that smelled of solvents. I used my nigh-unbreakable nails to undo the bolts and lower myself into the room.

"I can't see a thing," Dermot said in my ear. It sounded like shouting.

"I can."

My nose had been right. I was in a small, windowless room full of brooms and solvents and extra paper towels and toilet paper. I slowly turned the doorknob and cracked open the door. Empty hallway. There were no sounds, so I sneaked out. The walls were painted a bright, disconcerting green. I assumed Saskatchewan Oil Sands had used green here to paint a perfect relationship with nature. Green seemed to show up on almost every oil company's commercials.

I sneaked along, keeping an eye out for cameras. And big, mean men with guns. The carpet was thick enough to keep my movements quiet, and I made good headway. The fluorescent light provided an alternate-reality brightness. A guard came around the corner, but at the last second I heard his footsteps and skittered up the wall and clung to the ceiling behind a bank of fluorescent lights. I pressed myself to the ceiling as tightly as I could, trying to channel my inner ceiling tile. He would have seen me if he'd looked up, but it is surprising how many people never do that. Plus, only one fluorescent tube was working, casting a nice shadow over me.

When the guard got closer, I realized he wasn't a man. And when I saw the metal hands, I remembered my friend Naomi from the Antarctic compound.

"Impressive climb," Dermot said. "I nearly threw up."

I wanted to shout at him to shut up but bit my tongue. Naomi stopped below me and stood there for a moment. She'd heard something. I knew Dermot was just trying to be entertaining, but it was clearly the wrong time for that. My nails were slowly slipping out of the ceiling. Sweat began to form on my forehead.

Naomi looked left, right and behind her, then shrugged and kept walking.

"Just kidding about throwing up," Dermot said.

Naomi came to a sudden stop and glanced around again. The angle was still in my favor as long as she didn't look up.

After several long seconds she continued down the hall. "She heard that," I subvocalized.

"That's not possible."

"Well, she stopped twice, so it is possible."

"That's good to know. I'll keep communication to necessary information only. My apologies."

"Apology accepted." Believe me, I enjoyed subvocalizing that.

I landed silently on the floor, walked ahead and peeked around the next corner. This hall had a window partway down that would give a view into an interior room, which meant it was most likely an office. Oddly, I didn't see a door. What kind of office has just a window? Was it so the boss could watch his workers? Maybe the door was around the next corner.

I crept along the hallway and stopped next to the window. There was light coming out. I edged into position to get a better view. The room was not an office at all. Instead it looked like an apartment with a bed, a kitchenette, a small television and a rocking chair with a full bookshelf beside it. There was another window across the way.

Who the hell would put an apartment in the middle of a building and have a window for anyone to stare into? And who would want to read in the middle of that apartment in the middle of nowhere?

I peeked in the window. It was slowly dawning on me what this room was for.

A face appeared only a few inches away. It was my face looking back at me.

But older.

My mother was staring right at me. And she was fixing her hair.

Thirty-One
A ROOM FULL OF OBSERVATIONS

"MOM," I SAID. My voice was ragged but clear.

My mother. Nigella Fang. She was right there, and she didn't hear me. Nor did she appear to see me, even though I was a few inches away from her. She continued to fix her hair. It was in a style similar to what I remembered, that one gray streak running down her left temple. She looked healthy and perhaps just a pinch older. It had been three years since she'd disappeared. Three years! But seeing her brought back a flood of memories, a tsunami of emotion. My mom was right here!

My heart had stopped beating. One side of my brain forgot where I was standing, the danger I was in. This wasn't real. It was a dream. I'd imagined this moment countless times.

Why didn't you tell me about my sister? I wanted to shout. Or my father for that matter. But those were questions I could ask at a much later time.

She still couldn't see me. Had she gone blind?

"Mom," I said a bit louder.

"It's a mirrored window, Amber," Dermot whispered in my ear, making me shudder. "That's why she's not responding."

It creeped me out a bit that he was so much a part of this intimate moment. My mom was in a home designed to observe her. Like an animal in a zoo.

"She's beautiful," Dermot added. "Now I know where you get it from."

What an odd time to give me a compliment. "Yes, she is," I said.

Mom was doing a check for wrinkles around her eyelids. There were dark patches under her eyes, suggesting she hadn't been getting sleep. Her cheeks were a bit thinner, but overall she looked like she'd been fed properly.

"I just can't believe it," I said. "Mom's right here."

"You need to stop talking aloud," Dermot said. "Snap back to where you are, soldier." He said this last line sharply. "Gather your senses, Amber. We have to figure out what to do next."

"I'm not leaving her here," I said. "Never again!" I instinctively banged on the window. It was thick glass and only made the dullest thud. Mom looked a bit closer at the mirror.

"I don't expect you to leave her," Dermot said. "Stop banging though! We are going to get her out of there. The three of us will work our way into the compound. So sit tight until—"

Mom banged on the glass. It had to be bulletproof. She obviously knew it was a two-way mirror and perhaps had

BETRAYAL

long given up caring who saw her through it. She banged it again with both fists.

"Oh no," Dermot said. "Is there any way to get her to stop?"

"No," I said. "I think I better help her out."

"Wait," he said. But it was too late.

I smacked the glass, and Mom looked shocked and narrowed her eyes. I didn't know what was going through her head. Likely, she thought someone was just taunting her. But with the noise she was making, she would attract the attention of security any moment now. If they weren't already on the way.

I pulled back my fist and smashed it against the glass. It felt as though I'd shattered my hand, but a crack appeared.

"Amber!" Dermot shouted. I couldn't stop. I hit it again. Mom backed away. Another punch and the cracks broke so that about six inches of glass fell away. Two more quick hits and I smashed out a hole as large as my head.

"Who's there?" Mom said. It was so absolutely wonderful to hear her voice.

"Mom. It's me. Amber. It's me!"

She squinted through the hole, and I moved so we were face-to-face. "Amber! My dear, dear girl. I...I can't believe it. How did you find me?"

"That's a long story. But I'm getting you out of there. I'm—"

An alarm sounded, ringing like the bells of hell. I cringed and put up a hand to cover one ear. The hallway lights began to flash. I grabbed a corner of the window and pulled back, even though my hands were getting cut. I only came away with another inch. It would take hours at this pace.

"Mom! Give me a hand!" She pounded at the other side, knocking off another inch or two of glass. Her hands were soon bloody.

Something clunked behind her, and I saw the door on the other side of the room open, and three men in black fatigues jumped in. They raised their short-barreled guns and shot her. Mom shuddered and started to slip, holding onto the window with one hand.

"Run, Amber," she said, her voice already slow. "They've hit me with a sleep toxin." A dart darted through the window, missing my ear by less than an inch. "Run, Amber, rrrrun!" she drawled.

"Listen to her," Dermot said. "Get out of there!"

But I was enraged. There was my mother, right in front of me. I banged again and again. She turned and faced the security team, raised her hands as if she were going to tear out their throats, and leaped. Another dart hit her in midair, and she smacked onto the floor and skidded into a chair. She didn't get up.

Two of the men quickly dragged her away by the hair and one arm. The third one fired live rounds at me. They ricocheted off the glass, sprayed through the hole and peppered the wall behind me. I jumped back.

The last image I saw was them dragging Mom from the room.

BETRAYAL

"No!" I shouted. "No!"

Which is when a cannonball hit me.

I was knocked sideways and thrown down the hall, smacking into a wall, breaking the drywall and cracking my head. A blur of fists smacked me, and I was too slow to raise a hand. There was a horrible tightening around my throat.

It was metal queen Naomi staring down. She projected calmness, as if she were just peeling potatoes and not choking the last bit of life out of me. It became clear she was pressing on my carotid and trying to cut off the oxygen to my brain. Blackness was already in my skull and creeping over my thoughts.

I tried to push back, but the grip of her metal hands couldn't be broken. I brought up my foot and worked it into place against her chest, and then, using all my leg strength, I forced her off me.

She nearly took my esophagus with her, but she smacked into the wall with a satisfying (for me) sound. I got at least half of my wits back.

"There's a soldier to your left," Dermot said, and I pulled back just as three darts flew through the air and embedded in the wall. I spun and ran along the wall, and then my foot met his head, and the soldier was down.

Using darts meant they knew who I was now. And they wanted to capture me.

Everybody wanted my damn ovaries!

Naomi came flying through the air, but I caught her by the hand and, using a wushu move, tossed her

ARTHUR SLADE

through another wall. We were doing more damage than a wrecking crew.

She was right back up and at 'em. Well, at me. She obviously knew jujitsu, because suddenly I was flying. I hit the window that led into Mom's apartment, and it shattered around me. I landed inside the room and skittered across the floor, being cut in a thousand places. None of them seemed to be gushing, at least.

Naomi made a nice dive through the window, did an impressive flip and landed on her feet.

"Oh, it's so good to see you again," said a familiar voice in the wall. "My algorithms did not predict this. You are outside my calculations. I will have to adjust."

"Hector, my favorite AI," I said.

Then Naomi was on me. And I struck back, smashing into the wall of books. Mom is a reader, just like me. Though she has a taste for the classics. Dickens flew past. I picked up a hardback of *A Tale of Two Cities* and smacked Naomi across the jaw.

"Keep the AI talking," Dermot said.

I wanted to ask why. I also wanted to point out that I had my hands full. "What's in it for you, Hector? You must have better things to do than hang out with all these humans. Even this cyborg." I blocked a blow and hopped back.

"Good work," Dermot said.

"I do twenty thousand things at once," Hector explained. "This is just one of them. And I—oh, I see. You want me to talk. And you're receiving communication."

BETRAYAL

"Amber, I'm going to—" Dermot started, but then there was a high-pitched electronic screech in my ear that only stopped when I threw the earbud out.

"That should do it," Hector said. "So you have at least one accomplice."

"He's back in the States," I said.

"Short-wave communication. I recognize it."

Naomi had a hold of me, and those damn hands were tight. I remembered that the metal went partway up her arm.

"Just take it easy," she said. "We aren't going to hurt you."

"Yes, listen to her," Hector said. "We're on your side."

But I caught her hand, then lifted my leg and pushed her away from me at the same time as I held her hand. Naomi's eyes widened.

"Stop it! Stop it!" she said.

But I didn't stop. Her right hand broke off, shooting sparks and spraying blood. Her fingers were still clutching my own, but she flew back. Naomi managed to stand, despite the blood loss and what must have been incredible pain. But her reactions were slowed. I peeled her metal hand off me. She couldn't manage to bring her remaining hand up in time to block my blow. I hit her across the forehead with her own hand, and she crumpled to the floor. She didn't get up.

"Well, that was unfortunate," Hector said. "Those bionics are expensive. You are a naughty, naughty vampire."

I looked for a camera and saw something flashing in the ceiling. I threw Naomi's hand. It crashed into the camera like a missile. "Take that!" I said.

ARTHUR SLADE

"I have more than one camera," Hector said. "And more than one method to catch you. I was just delaying so I could do this."

I raised my hands and took a defensive stance. Nothing happened.

"What?" I asked.

"Oh, my timing is off," he said. "This, I mean! This!"

The door opened, and what looked like square, remote-controlled vacuums rolled in. "You're going to Roomba me to death?"

The little vacuum-shaped robots advanced, rolling over the glass and debris. They made clicking sounds, and about a hundred cables shot out faster than Indiana Jones's whip, looping around my arms, legs, torso and even my hair, and then attaching themselves to the wall and ceiling and floor, essentially stringing me up like a fly in a spider's web.

Why did these things keep happening to me?

Thirty-Two
A WONDERFUL SURPRISE

"THE KEY TO CAPTURING *Homo sapiens vampiris* is to avoid contact with the teeth," Hector explained. "Best not to use human antecedents." He paused, and I could almost hear his electronic gears clicking. "Intercedents, I mean."

"Wow, you sure like old, obsolete words." I didn't know if pretending to be brave in front of a computer made much sense.

"Yes, the joy of English. Numbers are always clearer and so ineffably perfect."

The cables were not much wider than the width of my finger. I yanked, trying to pull the Roomba things toward me, but they had extended grips into the floor. A guard came in and dragged Naomi out. A second guard picked up her hand.

"Well, Amber Fang, this is truly a wonderful surprise," Hector said. "I am as tickled pink as my nonexistent body can be. Serendipity has dipped us, for I have someone I'd like you to meet."

I stopped struggling long enough to breathe deeply. "Who?"

"My one and only master," Hector said without a hint of sarcasm.

The door opened, and a medium-sized white man in a black business suit walked in. He was bald, his face was plain, and his blue eyes were magnified behind his round glasses. "Hello," the man said. "I'm Anthony Zarc."

I was looking at the CEO, creator and president of ZARC Industries. Thousands of deaths could be traced directly to this man. I'd never seen a picture of him. Perhaps there weren't any in existence. To be honest, he didn't look like much, and I likely would have walked by him on the street without even a second glance. Except for his eyes. They measured me like no other human eyes could. A complete calmness. They were all-knowing eyes.

"Yes," Hector continued. "He's my Prometheus—the big cheese. The *numero uno*. The Machiavellian Mephistopheles."

"You won't speak about me that way, Hector," Anthony Zarc said softly. "You will be silent after you apologize."

"I am incredibly and completely sorry, sir," Hector said. There was contrition in his voice, and perhaps even fear. Could an AI feel fear? But the interaction gave me chills.

Zarc had not turned his eyes away from me for one microsecond. "It is a pleasure to have you as a guest, Amber Fang. I am sorry that you must be bound at this time."

"Then release me!" I said.

"I am sure you are aware that would be an unwise action. And I am a man who attempts to avoid unwise actions."

BETRAYAL

"Well, messing with my family is unwise." I was surprised at how much venom I was able to work into my voice. "What have you done with my mother?"

"She is being packaged for transport. Since the location of this lab is now known, we will be taking her to another safe place. The safest place, really. You will join us there and live with her."

"I have no intention of doing that." I didn't manage to say this with much gusto. It is hard to sound threatening when you are trapped.

"Intentions and reality are two different things," he said. "I do not want to cause you stress. You are such a fine specimen." I didn't like how he said that last word. "Your mother has been a great aid to us, though she would tell us nothing about you. She is an admirable mother. So the only information we have about you is from field agents' accounts and some blurry footage of your hit on my coworker Nathan Gabriel. And your shoe, of course. And a pinch of DNA we extracted from the scene." He breathed in, his all-measuring eyes looking me up and down. I felt naked before his gaze. "To see you in the flesh is overwhelming." He pushed his glasses up. He seemed so calm that it was hard to believe anything could overwhelm him. He was nonplussed to the core.

"I can't say I'm feeling the same sense of joy at seeing you."

"That is understandable. As you can see, your mother has been treated well."

"This looks like a fancy prison cell."

He shrugged. "Others would have put her in a modern-day iron maiden to extract every last string of DNA, every last molecule of her flesh. I chose to be civilized. Yes, it is an enclosure, but there was entertainment. And conversation. Many a time did I talk to her. She is a fascinating woman, and I am certain you are equally fascinating. I look forward to the time when we can have similar long conversations."

Again a horrible chill went down my spine. "It sounds like hell to me."

"Even your father is an interesting conversationalist, if one is patient."

"You have my father too?" I asked.

He nodded. "Yes, we acquired him from the League. I am pleased you didn't inherit his temperament. But he is an exceedingly intelligent man."

"He's not a man. He's a vampire."

He shook a finger at me, like a professor who'd caught a student making a mistake. "That's where you're wrong, Amber Fang. We're all from the same genetic tree. Or else you'd be of no use to me."

"Are you going to talk me to death? What are your intentions?"

"To use your genetic source material to create a master race." He said this without even a sign of irony or sarcasm. One would expect a *mwahahaha*, at the very least. "I deal in wars. In death. Imagine a soldier with recombinant DNA of a *Homo sapiens vampiris* combined with Naomi's hands. Her bionics. With Hector's mind. A soldier who only feeds once a month. With such tools, I will decide who wins wars. Whose special-ops teams complete their missions. And the price, well, the price will be high."

"Why my genetic material?" I asked.

"You perhaps already know that your kind is suffering from reproductive difficulties. The process I use needs reproductive material. Fertile material. You and your mother are the only two I've found."

"How on earth could you know whether or not I'm fertile?"

"I read the League's report on you."

My eyes widened. "They have a report on my fertility?"

"I've memorized the files. After your interrupted feeding, they brought food to you. When you ate that food, you fell into unconsciousness—all parts of your system being reset. But while you were out, they did a full test on your body."

I didn't know what to say. The League had implanted a tracker. But even worse, they had poked around in my insides and somehow tested my fertility. It was becoming hard to be upset that they'd been dismantled and destroyed.

"I know. It must be such an intrusion." His voice lacked even an iota of empathy. "You vampires are rightfully sensitive about your privacy. But you can conceive, Amber. Both thought and child."

As he talked, I stretched as hard as I could, searching for some give in the wires around me, but they only tightened. If I relaxed, they pulled even harder. Obviously, ZARC had perfected a way to capture vampires.

"So you found my mother all those years ago?"

He nodded. "Yes. I designed an algorithm that predicted her feeding patterns. We were supposed to get both of you, but your mother wouldn't let us know your location. She's a determined woman. I assume that's a trait she passed down to you. I am truly pleased to have you here, but sorrowed that it is against your will."

"Then let me go. Be a gentleman about it."

That got a slim smile. "The reality is you are needed and necessary, Amber. You will be treated better by me than you would have been by your brethren had they captured you. So I will take a small moral comfort in that. The investors expect results, and I deliver them. I regret that it's time for you to go now." He made a signal with his hand, circling a finger. Whether the command was for Hector or someone else, I wasn't certain. The result was that four black-clad men came in, their high-tech dart guns raised. "You will be transported in comfort and safety, and when you awaken, you'll be reunited with your mother in a comfortable room. That's a promise. I imagine you've missed her."

I began to strain, pulling each muscle tight. I yanked so hard that finally, finally one of the cables snapped.

Zarc made another signal, and the men fired. In that same moment I was able to adjust my position just enough to dodge the darts and whip the cable out within an inch of his ear. He didn't blink. He certainly was a calm son of a bitch.

The cable snapped into one of the men, knocking him back. But not before he fired. A dart stuck into my right leg,

BETRAYAL

and I felt a familiar freezing sensation. The other two guards adjusted their aim. I began to pull back my metal whip, knowing I didn't have enough time to stop them.

The wall burst open behind me, and plaster came flying in. I turned to see a blur of metal arms and legs. Dermot, clad in his exoskeleton, was crashing through the wires, snapping them with his weight and momentum. Half the cables had broken, which allowed me to plant my good leg and tear away the remaining metal lines. My right leg was full of pins and needles, but I stood straight.

"Intruder alert," Hector said.

"I can see that," Anthony Zarc answered.

The soldiers fired their darts, and I rolled across the floor and whipped out my cable again, pulling the gun from one's hand. The third guard had drawn a pistol and raised it, but before he could get off a shot, a crossbow bolt *thwucked* into his forehead.

Derek and Steph were crouched behind the last bit of the collapsed wall, holding crossbows.

Which left Anthony Zarc all alone in the middle of the room. Looking at me, then over at Dermot. A very small smile appeared on his face.

"Looks like you're going to be our prisoner," I said, leaping, mostly using my left leg for power.

I went right through him and smacked into the floor. I turned to see that Zarc was standing right where he'd been, looking down at me. He had either moved at an impossible speed or...

"I'm a hologram," he said. He looked so much like he was there, even the fluorescent reflected in his eyes. We were reflected in his eyes. "The risk ratio of allowing physical harm to come to my person was unacceptable. It has been pleasant to chat, but this conversation is finished." Even as a projection, he projected pure competence.

"We have to go, Amber," Dermot said. He was sweating in that exoskeleton.

"Not without my mother," I said.

"It's too late to get her," Zarc said. "She is gone. But the invitation to join her is open. You are welcome to come with me. And you too, Dermot. I would like to have conversations with you."

"He's just delaying us," Dermot said.

I saw a glint in the ceiling and spotted the smallest projector. I leaped up and smashed it, making Zarc disappear.

His voice wasn't gone though. "You are surrounded," Zarc said. "Your safest option is to seat yourself on the floor and assume a nonthreatening position with hands behind your head."

"It's another delaying tactic," Dermot said. "Let's go."

I followed him back through the hole he'd plowed in the wall. We ran down the hall.

"They'll be expecting us to go out the way we came in," Dermot said. He *thunked* along. A security guard appeared in front of us and was downed by a crossbow bolt before I could make a move. Derek and Steph were rather efficient.

BETRAYAL

"Are you my knight in shining armor?" I asked.

"Just a concerned citizen," he said. Perhaps he was getting healthier, but running was obvious exertion for him, even though the exoskeleton was doing all the work. "We'll go out here." He pointed, then turned to the left, ducked his head like a football player and smashed into the exterior wall. He went right through, making a Dermot-sized hole. I ran up to it. He'd landed on the ground and was now waving back at us. We followed. I leaped, and the others, perhaps more wisely, scaled down the side of the wall.

A *thup*, *thup*, *thup* caught my attention. It was too large to be a drone. A black helicopter on the top of another building above us began rotating its blades. The angle was low enough for me to see three security guards rushing Zarc to the door. The real man.

"That has to be him," I said. "No point in rushing a hologram to a helicopter. We can end this now."

"It's too far, Amber," Dermot said. "There are too many sight lines."

As if to prove his point, someone began firing at us. I crouched, and Dermot stepped between me and the shooter.

"You're not Iron Man," I said. "Those bullets can kill you."

"This way!" He pointed. "That's the shortest distance to the woods and to cover."

He began to run, and I followed almost automatically. But I did take a moment to glance back at the helicopter. Anthony Zarc, the real Anthony Zarc, was watching us from his perch on top of the building. His arms were crossed.

ARTHUR SLADE

But what I saw behind him caught my complete attention.

Four men were carrying one of those metal eggs toward the helicopter. I knew my mother was in that egg.

I changed direction and ran straight for the helicopter.

Thirty-Three
AN EGG IN HAND

I DIDN'T LOOK TO SEE IF Dermot was following. For all I knew, he and the others had kept running toward the woods. I charged at full speed, zagging and zigging to avoid any potential bullets. My eyes were completely focused on that egg. Yes, it could have been one last trap, but I doubted even Zarc could put a trap together this quickly. Zarc himself didn't move.

The men had tossed a webbing over the egg and were tightening belts, attaching it to the helicopter. The adrenaline must have fought off whatever agent they'd had in the darts, because both my legs were working perfectly now. I crossed half the distance in a few seconds, gaining momentum.

Then I heard a buzzing and got the sense that something was coming toward me in the darkness. A drone. I had no idea how it was armed and couldn't even see it yet, but the noise meant it was close. So I leaped as high as possible, and before it could fire, I smashed it from the sky. I landed, rolled and kept running.

Which is when Anthony Zarc turned away from me and walked toward his helicopter. I raced up to the wall of the building and climbed at a speed even I didn't know I was capable of. Bullet holes began to appear next to me. And I had enough wits remaining to climb to the left, then right, then jump up ten feet—all so I wasn't an easy target.

I leaped over the balustrade, and the guards started *pop, pop, popping* their firearms, all of which I avoided with a slide that a baseball star would be proud of.

I took one guard out with a thrown brick. Another was near enough that a flying kick silenced both him and his gun. But there were five, and that meant three too many for me.

The third fell, a crossbow bolt in his chest.

The fourth shot me. Right in the arm. But I didn't stop. I was pumped full of adrenaline, and all I could see was the egg and that the helicopter was taking off. The egg had been attached to the bottom, so it looked like some insect queen about to give birth. I knocked the fourth guard's head back. And the fifth fell when a bolt hit his chest.

The helicopter was already ten feet in the air, the wind from the rotors pushing me back. The windows were black, so I couldn't see my enemy.

I jumped, arcing toward it, bleeding, screaming— an arrow of anger—and clung to the egg. I ripped at the belt and webbing that held it in place. But there were too many. The helicopter went higher. Higher. And I pulled and pulled.

BETRAYAL

Then a *thunk*. Dermot was beside me, clinking in his suit and pushing, prying and tearing with his metallic arms. Then there was a long *rip*, and both of us fell from the helicopter.

We landed on the roof, the egg still above us, wobbling.

Then it fell too.

But Dermot caught it, the weight driving him to his knees.

The helicopter raced away, silent now. There was a rifle firing from one of the concrete towers, so we fled across the roof, found a set of stairs and ran toward the woods. Dermot carried the egg under one arm. It looked like something we'd stolen from a giant magical duck.

We raced into the branches and bush and didn't stop running for what seemed like hours. The whole time, I kept my ears open for the sound of drones. Or a helicopter. Or any pursuit at all.

Finally Dermot made a signal, and we stopped. Derek and Steph took up positions on either side of us, looking ahead and back.

Dermot set the egg on the ground. Surprisingly, it was only partially damaged. The gauges were dark. I pushed on the buttons. The damn gauges weren't lit up, and I worried that whatever processes were keeping Mom alive in there had stopped. She could have suffocated.

In a clearing, under the pale light of the moon, I tore off the front door.

A man was sleeping peacefully inside. A very familiar-looking man. He opened his eyes and looked directly at me.

"Oh, it's you, Amber," he said. "Be a good girl and wake me in a few hours." Then my father closed his eyes and went back to sleep.

I had no words.

No damn words at all.

Thirty-Four
THE ONLY REMAINING SAFE HOUSE

AN EXTRA FIFTY THOUSAND in American dollars convinced the pilot to remove two of the seats so that we could jam the egg into the back of the plane. He also agreed to take us to a different destination. Soon we were in the air, and Dermot was reading coordinates to the pilot.

"It's the last safe house," he explained to me a few minutes later. There was a sickening feeling in my gut, a sensation of anger that boiled there. I had been so close to Mom, I had almost touched her, and now instead of her I had this obscenity of a creature—my father. He would kill me in a heartbeat if it served his purposes. But perhaps he knew something about where they were taking Mom. That was the only reason I was keeping him alive.

Dermot looked paler than he had before and much smaller now that he'd removed the exoskeleton. But there was, perhaps, the slightest tinge of pink to his cheeks. Either it was leftover blood or he was healing.

We traveled south, stopping only for fuel. Eventually we landed at a military base in Alberta, where we said goodbye to our pilot and to Derek and Steph. Dermot, my father and I were transported to a military transport plane. I didn't even ask what our destination was. Without more than a minute's delay, the plane's engines fired up, and we were in the air again.

"We'll find a way to get her back," Dermot said. He put his hand on mine. To my surprise, it felt warm. "I promise you."

I said nothing. We flew south. Away from the prairies. Away from the mess we'd left behind.

I truly hoped he'd keep his promise.

READ AN EXCERPT FROM **AMBER FANG BOOK 3: REVENGE**.

One

BLOOD IN THE SAND

MY FIRST GOAL was to not spill any blood in the sand.

Placencia is a small fishing village in Belize with an odd mix of tired, quaint buildings and fancy new tourist digs made of faux palm trees and glass. The beach is not much more than a strip, yet it's beautiful, and there's a lovely view of the Caribbean Sea. The tourists were generally happy, the locals had genuine smiles, and the weather was calm.

It was a shame I was hunting a murderer here.

A shame but totally necessary. A girl has got to eat.

The sand on the beach squished pleasurably between my toes. The palm trees waved pleasantly above me. The air was stinking hot, but I'd taken the precaution of slathering on an SPF 45 suntan lotion, from my feet to my forehead. The sun won't kill me, but vampires burn easily—well, the pale ones do. I wore a black one-piece swimsuit and a lovely straw hat.

The man I was going to eat had just lowered his chiseled and tattooed body onto a red towel. Those tattoos would be used to identify his corpse later. He was Grigoriy Belyakov and, as you can guess by his name, he was Russian. Not ballet-loving Russian. But more the Kalashnikov-firing, vodka-loving type. Someone has to be the stereotype.

He was also a high-level employee of ZARC Industries and the key to where my mother had been taken. There were at least twenty people—from journalists to envoys to bystanders—who had been killed by this hit man. And he obviously was experiencing no regrets for those murders. In fact, he'd just finished several regret-free sangrias before heading to the beach.

He was exactly the type of man my mother, Nigella Fang, would approve of—for eating, that is. She had taught me to have only ethical meals. It is how vampires should behave. Apparently, she and I are in the minority as far as vampires are concerned. The rest of my relatives will eat any human they can sink their teeth into. They are so gauche.

I'd followed Grigoriy from his cabin and had been keeping my eye on him over the last twenty-four hours. As far as I could tell, he was alone here, which suggested he was truly on holiday. He adjusted his sunglasses and, lo and behold, pulled out a book to read. I squinted, but I couldn't tell what the title was.

So he wasn't completely horrible. The fact he was a reader meant I'd be extra careful to not mess up the feeding part of this venture. That's my deal with murderers who have enough taste to be bookworms—no messy death!

Not that I am a naturally messy eater. But sometimes mess happens.

EXCERPT FROM REVENGE

I chose a shady spot several feet away, spread out my own towel, sat down and watched him closely. I even separated his heartbeat from all the sun-slowed heartbeats of the sunbathers around him. The breeze carried his scent my way, a pleasant cologne.

I watched.

And I watched.

The crashing waves and the heat were sleep inducing, and I hadn't been sleeping well since I'd seen my mom at a ZARC compound in Canada three months earlier. I thought I'd rescued her by grabbing a huge egg, but inside it, waiting like a scorpion, I'd found my father instead.

It was kind of like finding a dog turd inside a Christmas present.

Dad was still in that egg at a military base in Montana. Dermot had rejigged the dials and revamped the life-sustaining systems, and we were pretty sure my father would continue to live. I wanted Dad to stay on ice. Permanently, if necessary.

Dermot has been helping me track down Mom, but his resources have shrunk like Cinderella's pumpkins at midnight. He is basically all that is left of the once-powerful League, a group of do-gooders who wanted to rid the world of enemy agents. But they have been mostly wiped out by several ZARC hit teams.

Dermot was watching me watch the murderer. By that I mean Dermot was observing the scene with a drone that hovered at a very great height above this beach. I could just hear its rotors. No one else should be able to.

ARTHUR SLADE

Our big break came three weeks ago when I received a text that said: **From one book lover to another. A gift.** The image of Grigoriy was texted to me, along with a PDF of his hit-man background and a copy of his travel plans.

Is that you, Agnes? I'd texted back. There had been no reply.

There was also no way to trace the origin of the text. The number was just 000000000. There was no conceivable way for anyone to have my secret phone number other than Dermot. Yet the text had still arrived. Nothing Dermot did—and he went all geeky on it—could find the source.

I was certain the text had come from the Returns—the ninja librarians who had rescued me from my sister's clutches. Even the thought that such a thing as ninja librarians existed still seemed ludicrous. But I'd seen their glinting dart guns and deadly accurate crossbows. Their official name is the Preservational Librarians Guild, and their goal is to preserve human knowledge and civilization. But they also have a policy of not interfering with the day-to-day world.

Still, I was pretty sure the text had come from the one ninja librarian who'd disobeyed their policies to give me information about Mom's location. Agnes. I could still see her dark, friendly face. I'd only said a few words to her.

But she knew me intimately. She was a Fanger—apparently there is a faction of librarians who follow my exploits using metadata and information sweeps and...well, who knows what. But they call themselves Fangers.

I still blush when I think of that. I have *fans*!

EXCERPT FROM REVENGE

Fanger fans!

I was certain the reasons behind the text would come clear once I'd eaten Grigoriy.

Two blissful hours passed. I read. Snoozed with one eye open. The drone hovered.

My current read was *Life of Pi*, which seemed perfect for the beach—it was easy to fall into a novel about a boy trapped on a boat with a tiger when I could hear the waves only a few feet away. My only complaint was there wasn't enough bloodletting in the book. I found myself identifying with the tiger far too closely.

I must have snoozed with both eyes closed. When I opened them again, *Pi* was in the sand and Grigoriy was gone.

But it was a beach, and he'd left tracks, so I followed them. Oddly enough, I could tell that he'd walked right past me—dangerously close—but that could have been because the beach was so crowded and he'd been forced to take that path.

He had wandered over to one of the open bamboo huts set up with tables for Ping-Pong, foosball and other games for the tourists. The one he'd chosen had a pool table, and I heard the *crack, crack* of balls smashing into each other. I spotted him leaned over the table, sizing up his next shot. He seemed to be almost angry at the balls.

Death would soothe that anger.

I scanned the surrounding area to be sure no one was watching or nearby. Four posts held the roof above the table, and the walls were only hip high—the rest was open air.

The walls would block any action once I had him on the ground. And I didn't need much more than two minutes to feed.

He was facing away from me, so I sneaked up the stairs without making a sound and slipped in behind him. He began to turn, perhaps had sensed my presence, but I clamped my hand on his shoulder and flipped him onto his back so hard that it drove the air out of his lungs, and the balls on the table popped up and down. I landed on him, with my knees on either side of his chest.

He snarled something in Russian and reached out with his meaty arms to choke me but was surprised when I grabbed them and easily pushed them back down. I licked my lips and noted that there was an octopus tentacle tattooed around his neck. The rest of the octopus, presumably, covered his back.

"We'll be conversing in English," I said. "Get it?"

He narrowed his thick eyebrows and replied, "Yes. I speak English."

"Good. You work for ZARC, right?"

"ZARC? Vhat is this ZARC?" He smiled as he said this.

"Don't play games. You're only half as clever as you think. You have information I need, and you'll give it to me. Now."

"Vhat information do you be needing?"

"There is a woman in your care, Nigella Fang. Do you know her?"

His smile widened. "Ov course, she's big bride."

"Bride?"

"Pride, is dat da word?"

EXCERPT FROM REVENGE

"Pride?" Jesus, we were doing an Abbott and Costello routine.

"Prize," he said finally. "Big prize. I don't like your English words."

"Well, you won't like this either," I said, pressing my right knee into his chest. "I want you to tell me exactly where she's located. I need to find her."

"Dey know you are looking for her. You will not find her. You vill die."

"Thanks for the vote of confidence," I said. I pushed my knee even harder into his chest. "Anyway, you're here to help." He tried to get up, and I slammed him down. "I don't want to be testy about it, but I will break things. Things that are part of you."

"I've had everyting broken," he said.

Oh, that would make it harder to threaten him. And I didn't know if I could truly torture someone by snapping fingers or pulling off extremities. But as far as a comeback, all I came up with was, "You've never been questioned by a vampire. I'll go all medieval on your ass."

Grigoriy chuckled. I was starting to hate this man. He just wasn't taking me seriously enough.

Then...footsteps.

I snapped my head to the side, expecting to find an accomplice with an AK-47. Dermot was watching from a drone, but he was at least three minutes away if he ran fast.

Our visitor was a pake-skinned woman in an orange bikini. "Oh, sorry," she said.

I slipped my hand over Grigoriy's mouth so he couldn't talk. He bit me, but I didn't pull my hand away.

"I haven't seen him for months," I said, adding a conspiratorial wink. "I just couldn't help myself. He looks good enough to eat." She grinned, gave me the thumbs-up and backed away.

We were alone again.

I yanked my hand away from his mouth. He'd actually drawn blood. "Don't bite me! I'll bite *you*."

But in that moment of distraction, he had grabbed my shoulder and, in an impressive wrestling move, he shifted me to the side, slammed me down and somehow got on top of my back, forcing my face into the sandy floor.

I twisted my head, because it's always important to see your opponent. Grigoriy was grinning and perfectly at ease. He reached quickly into his hair and pulled out a long filament that glittered slightly. It had two little knobs on either end.

What the hell?

Its purpose became clear when he put it around my neck and began to twist.

A garrote. He'd somehow tied it into his short hair. Nice trick that, I thought, as I began to choke.

ARTHUR SLADE is a Governor General's Award–winning author of many novels for young readers, including the graphic novel *Modo: Ember's End*, which is based on characters from *The Hunchback Assignments* trilogy, and *Death by Airship* in the Orca Currents collection. Raised on a ranch in the Cypress Hills of Saskatchewan, Arthur now makes his home in Saskatoon, Saskatchewan.

SINK YOUR TEETH INTO THE ENTIRE AMBER FANG SERIES.

AMBER HAS A THIRST FOR KNOWLEDGE. *And blood.*

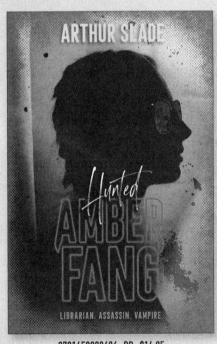

Librarian by day, vampire assassin by night, Amber Fang dines only on delicious, cold-blooded killers. But one day she walks into a trap, and suddenly the hunter becomes the hunted. Then she receives a job offer that sounds too good to be true. Someone wants to pay her to kill the world's worst criminals.

9781459822696 PB $14.95

"Imagine Buffy the Vampire Slayer — except Buffy is the vampire and has the research skills of Giles."

—Kirkus Reviews

"A romp of a read... so much fun!"

—Susin Nielsen, *author of*
WE ARE ALL MADE OF MOLECULES *and* **OPTIMISTS DIE FIRST**

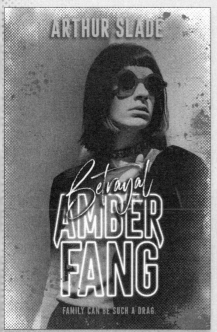

9781459822726 PB $14.95

Amber discovers that a powerful top-secret organization is behind her mother's disappearance. She travels around the world, battling cyborgs and bad-guy vampires in an attempt to rescue her mom.

Amber finally faces off against ZARC, the secret arms-dealing organization that has captured her mother. Then ZARC strikes a blow that leaves Amber stunned and heartbroken. Now she's out for revenge.

9781459822757 PB $14.95